HOT STUFF

HOT AS PUCK

BOOK ONE

RHIAN CAHILL

Hot Stuff
Hot as Puck Book One
By Rhian Cahill

For more information visit:
www.rhiancahill.com

For the characters that have been in my head sharing bits and pieces of their stories for years. Finally, I've got you on the page.

To Mr.C. You held my hand, you stood beside me, without you the battle would have been harder to fight.
#fuckcancer

WALKER

"C'mon, don't be shy, show me the goods."

I'm pretty sure the curl of my lips is not the cocky smirk I'm going for but when I drop my jeans, the smile I couldn't muster two seconds ago blooms bright when the woman in front of me chokes on a sucked-in breath and lowers her camera.

Her gaze is glued to what I've revealed. It takes her a minute before she gulps—hard—averts her eyes and stammers, "W-where are the, ah, your, um"—she waves a hand in the direction of my groin as she swallows again—"*underwear?*"

Keeping her gaze averted, she scans the room and I study her. She isn't bad looking. Actually, she's kind of hot and could easily be on this side of the camera but my dick didn't even twitch when she was looking at it.

One more thing to blame on Kristina, the woman I once thought I might spend my life with. Over the last year she systematically killed any possibility of forever we had right along with my libido.

This morning's events dealt the final blow to my tolerance of her drama.

And that was before I sat in the doctor's office and had the professional life I had planned from the age of four completely derailed.

Fuck my life. The whole thing is screwed.

Personal. Professional. Nothing is the way I thought it would be at this point in time.

Whatever relationship I had with Kristina was over months ago, and my career took the final blow today.

The bubble of hope I've been living in burst completely during today's appointment.

I can't deny it any longer.

As soon as news gets out, I'll be lucky to keep this sponsorship deal, never mind fucking it up by flashing my dick at the photographer.

I'm reaching down for my pants when I hear, "All right, hot stuff, put that thing away."

I can't see the person behind the voice because of the studio lights, but the voice alone gets a reaction below the belt I haven't felt in over a year.

"You always go commando, hot stuff?"

Clearing my throat, I answer, "No." I don't elaborate; there's no way I'm offering up the reason for my lack of underwear. "This is a shoot for compression shorts, right?"

I'll be honest. I figured the fact I had no clean briefs and this sponsorship being for Rogue's latest athletic underwear line, turning up commando wouldn't matter.

Clearly I should have asked where the merchandise was before dropping my pants.

"Yes, sorry I'm late." I can hear amusement in the words as well as movement behind the glare of lights but still have no visual of the owner of that sexy rasp. "Although it was totally worth the perv."

Shit! What the fuck am I doing?

Scrambling to pull up my jeans, I barely get them past my thighs when the hottest woman I've ever seen—and believe me when I say I've seen plenty of hot women, but this one...*Jesus fucking Christ...*—comes strolling into view.

In a split second that below the belt quiver goes from a mild tremor to a house-crumbling quake. And that floppy disinterested muscle between my legs turns into a flagpole.

If you Google the phrase 'sex on legs', you'll get a screen filled with the vision walking toward me.

Fuck!

I cup my junk, needing both hands to cover the no longer flaccid appendage—the one that has deserted me in recent months but now shows up in all its glory.

I feel like a teenager with an unfortunate case of hormone overload.

The knowing smirk on the stunning face in front of me doesn't help me at all. That sexy tilt of her lips makes me want to kiss her until we're both stupid.

Hell. I'm already there. Stupid as any pre-pubescent boy getting his first look at an in-the-flesh naked woman.

And this woman isn't naked!

"Tanya, you mind giving us a few minutes?" the wet dream getting closer to me by the second asks.

I hear movement, figure the photographer is leaving us alone, but I can't take my eyes off the woman bringing my body back to life when only moments ago I thought it was dead.

I need to pull up my pants but I don't dare take my hands off my dick for fear it'll stab one of us in the eye.

She gives me no choice but to let go when she stops two feet away and offers her hand. "Hello, Walker Alcott, it's a pleasure to meet you."

The twinkle in her eyes tells me she knows my predicament and sees the funny side of this encounter, but I can't be sure and, let's be real, this could be my last big paying job once the extent of my injury gets out.

Taking her hand, I say, "Pleasure to meet you too, Ms..."

"James. Oakley James."

Motherfucker. I flashed the goddamn CEO of Rogue!

"Ah, um." I clear my throat. "The owner of Rogue?"

"Guilty. Although I'm part owner. One quarter of KAW, the parent company of Rogue." She smiles and the twitching in my dick goes up a notch when images of those lips wrapped around it fill my head.

"Right. Okay." Letting go of her hand, I yank my jeans up one-handed, struggling to keep my dick covered with the other. "Sorry about that. I, um, had a laundry mishap this morning."

It's a lie. It was no mishap. Fucking Kristina took to every last pair of my briefs with scissors. Actually, she took to more than my underwear but that's beside the point.

Ms. James tips her head slightly to the right, a contemplative look on her face. "Can I ask you a personal question, Walker?"

"Ah, sure."

"How invested are you in your relationship?"

Relationship? I haven't been in a relationship for a year, the battle Kristina is waging couldn't be called one unless you're talking enemies at war.

And what the fuck? Is this woman reading my mind?

Shaking my head, I say, "I'm sorry?"

"Let's go over here and sit down."

Before I can argue or ask her to explain, she spins on her heel and heads back the way she came, disappearing behind the bright glare once again. Snapping out of my stupor, I button up my pants and follow.

By the time I get to where she's standing beside a small table with two chairs, I can see we are alone. I have no idea where the photographer went or if I'm even going to be doing a photo shoot anymore.

After dropping my jeans and flashing the photographer *and* Oakley James, the woman is probably preparing to tear up our contract.

"Take a seat," she offers as she sinks into one of her own.

My ass hits the chair, and I can't come up with anything to say other than, "Why do you want to know about my relationship? Not that I'm in one. And what does that have to do with me being the face of Rogue's newest athletic shorts?"

"Nothing. It has to do with this." She taps a large envelope on the table.

I shake my head again. This woman is confusing me at every turn. "I'm not following."

"You're based in New York right now."

"Yes," I answer, even though we both know it wasn't a question.

"Would you move?"

My spine stiffens. She can't know I'm about to be out of a job. Forced to retire due to injury. Sure the team could keep me on injured reserve for the rest of the season, but why would they when there's no hope I'll play competitive hockey again.

I swallow around the lump in my throat and ask, "Why would I move?"

She leans back in her chair and folds her arms over her chest, pushing her mouthwatering breasts higher, and it takes all my strength not to drop my gaze from hers.

My dick is twitching in my pants again too.

I don't get the reaction I'm having to Oakley James. Shit. Kristina stood naked in front of me numerous times in the last year of our relationship and got no response.

"I'm going to be honest here, Walker, and then we can talk about whether or not you would move."

I nod. I'm all for honesty from a woman. Especially after the lies I've heard pass from Kristina's lips in recent years.

Hell, maybe everything she ever said was a lie. At this point I wouldn't be surprised.

"I know it's highly unlikely you'll play in the NHL again."

My lungs fill with air so fast I choke. Covering my mouth

with a fist, I cough hard, giving myself a few seconds to digest the words she's just spoken.

They might be true but no one—including the many doctors I've seen over the last few months—has uttered those words out loud.

Until this morning.

And even then, they skirted around the truth, never once coming right out and saying "you'll never play professionally again."

"I don't know what the doctors are saying but from what has been made public and the fact you have not returned to the ice, it's obvious to me your professional playing career is over."

Fuck. Her words are like daggers through my chest. How can they have a greater impact coming from her lips when I'd felt nothing but numb when the doctor spoke similar words this morning?

"Here's where I ask you to sign an NDA." She slips a sheet of paper from beneath the envelope and hands it to me along with a pen. "You sign that, and we can really talk."

Glancing down, it takes me a moment to focus on the words. It's a standard Non-Disclosure Agreement. I have no idea what she could want to talk about that would require one and really, when I think about it, I should get her to sign one because if I tell her I'm out of the league before I tell anyone else, she could leak it to the press.

At this point though, it's inevitable the press will find out some time today, tomorrow at the latest. As soon as I'm finished here, I have to call Drake, my agent, and give him the news from the doctor so he can get on top of things with my team.

The team that won't be mine much longer.

"Okay," I say, and scribble my signature. "Talk."

"Would you move from New York if you had another career opportunity within the league?"

"Yes. Although I have no idea what I'd do if I can't play."

She smiles, a cat that got the canary smile. "Really? I find that hard to believe. Surely you've thought about what you'd do after you retire."

"Sure. But retirement is years away. At least ten."

"You saw yourself playing until thirty-nine? That's one hell of a career."

"It would be." Except…now it wouldn't. I can't stop the sigh that drops my shoulders and slumps me back in my chair.

"Before I tell you what that career could look like now, I want to revisit my original question. How invested are you in your relationship?"

"I'm not. It's done. Has been for a year."

"And yet she's still living in your apartment."

Fury rolls through me, snapping my spine straight. "She has never *lived* in my apartment. We maintained separate places throughout our three-year relationship, a relationship I ended a year ago."

"But she uses your address for all her bills and as her home address."

My teeth grind just thinking about how many times I reminded Kristina to change that shit back only to find out she took no notice of my demands. One of many things I said she ignored over the years we were together. "I never said she could and—"

"It sounds as though you've never been as deeply invested as your practice-wife."

"Practice-wife?"

"More honesty. I've had her investigated because when I offer you the opportunity I think you're the perfect fit for, I don't want her interfering with you saying yes. Or coming with you." She shakes her head. "No. I definitely don't want her coming with you. Everything my PI found reinforces my own conclusions. She's after the title of hockey wife and she's been attempting to steamroll you into being the hockey part of that title."

"Wow." I don't know what to address first. This mysterious offer or the fact she's had Kristina investigated. "A PI?"

"I take business seriously and what I'm planning will involve enough drama without your practice-wife tagging along for the ride."

"And what exactly do you have planned and how do I fit in?"

"First, how do you plan to ditch Kristina Bancroft?"

"At this point I haven't a clue. I took away her access to my apartment, hell, she's banned from the building, and I returned all her personal effects months ago, and yet she's still managing to fuck with my life. Hence my commando self."

Oakley's fingers drum on the envelope. "I'm sure there's a story there..."

"Honestly, it's not worth going into. Although I will be using a different laundry service from now on."

"I see. Well, when you say yes to my offer, you'll need to do that anyway." Flattening her palm on the envelope, she pushes it toward me. "This is going to get her out of your life. Use it however you see fit. It's my gift to you for hearing me out."

"I haven't heard anything yet."

"You will." She tips her head at the table. "Go on, open it."

This is one of the strangest conversations I've ever had but I can't deny I'm curious.

Reaching for the envelope, I flip it over, lift the flap, and peek inside. What I see makes me more intrigued.

"Photos?"

"Hmm." After that little hum that has my dick twitching again, she remains tight-lipped.

Shrugging, I reach in and pull the thick stack of pictures out. There are at least twenty of them, eight by ten in size.

The first one is hard to work out. Until I turn the pile to the right twice. Then...*holy shit!* "Is that...?" I squint at the image.

"If you're going to ask me if that's a profile shot of Jerry Cantrell, the very much married owner of the hockey team you're currently contracted to, then yes, it is." Oakley grins. "Take a look at the rest."

The next shot is a wider view of Jerry sitting on a bed. A bed with a headboard I have personally leaned against, not in over a year thankfully, but still. The man who is effectively my *married* boss is sitting on Kristina's bed.

Naked!

My gaze darts up to Oakley's. "How'd you get these?"

"Doesn't matter. All copies are in your hands and on the memory card in the envelope."

"And you're giving them to me? How are pictures of Jerry—"

"Keep going."

I flick to the next one and bile rises in my throat. "What the fuck is he putting in her ass?"

"It's called a butt plug."

"I know what a butt plug looks like, and this isn't it."

"I believe it's part of the whole 'pony play' thing they both seem to be into."

"Pony play?"

"Yes, it's a fetish, obviously. One partner wears a bridle and a plug that looks like a horse's tail so they—"

"Whoa, whoa, whoa." I drop the pictures on the table and put up both my hands. "I don't need to know that shit." *Fuck*. I'll need brain bleach or a full bottle of tequila to wipe that shit out of my head.

Laughing, Oakley reaches over and grabs the photos. "The only one you really need is this one." She shuffles through and finds the one she wants.

When she holds it out, I really don't want to look but again, curiosity gets me. Looking down, I see she's singled out a shot of Kristina riding Jerry. She is mid stride, either down or up, it doesn't matter; it shows all I need to finally get the woman to leave me the fuck alone.

"Okay. Thanks." I shove the stack of pictures back in the envelope. I can't stand looking at them any longer. I'll deal with them later and decide how to use them. "Now, what's this opportunity?"

"How would you like to coach the Baton Rouge Rogues?"

"Baton Rouge Rogues? What are they? A high school team?"

I've never heard of them. I can't even work out what kind of sports team she's referring to. All I know is it isn't in the National Hockey League.

"You know I play *ice* hockey, right?"

OAKLEY

"You know I play *ice* hockey, right?"

Walker's words have me laughing. "I'm aware," I manage to say.

"Sorry. I've never heard of the Baton Rouge Rogues."

"You and the rest of the country." I can't help the cocky smile that curls my lips. By the time I'm done, every hockey fan in the world will know who the Rogues are. And a good number of them will be cheering us on.

"Look, I don't know what you're hinting at. Why don't you just spell it out for me?"

Reaching into the briefcase at my feet, I pull out a thick stack of papers. Turning the bundle, I slap it on the table in front of Walker so he can read the cover page. "This is who the Baton Rouge Rogues are."

My voice is triumphant because I feel victorious.

We did it.

We're *doing* it.

As of this morning, KAW became the owner of the National Hockey League's expansion franchise. And the Rogues became the only female owned and run hockey team in the league.

And the first order of business, after putting the proposal

together and winning the bid for this new franchise, is to secure the head staff. Our GM and assistant coach are already locked in.

Now I just have to convince Walker Alcott that head coach of the Rogues is what he wants.

What he needs.

"When did the league announce the new franchise?"

"They haven't yet. The official press conference takes place later this month."

"But this is—"

"Yes. That's the contract between KAW and the league for that franchise. Hence the NDA."

"You." He shakes his head. "This is crazy. Baton Rouge?"

A grin splits my face.

"No one is going to believe a hockey franchise in Baton Rouge is going to be successful."

"They're wrong. We"—I wave my hand between us—"are going to *make* them wrong."

"How do I factor into this?"

"You're going to lead the team—"

"I can't"—he swallows hard—"I can't play."

"I don't want you to *play*." Leaning forward, I lock my gaze with his. "I want you to *coach*."

He nods, his gaze turning thoughtful. "Who have you got lined up for head coach?"

I have to laugh. This man, with all his skills as a player, a strategist, a competitor, can't see his place on this team is not to assist. "You."

His genuine shock keeps the smile on my face. I've known from the moment I heard about Walker's injuries, he was our man and, when I talked it over with Blake and Nat, they agreed with me.

Cami doesn't have an opinion; she doesn't even really like sport. Other than watching Blake play over the years, I'm pretty sure my best friend hasn't been to a sporting event in her life.

Before we'd locked on to Walker for our head coach, we'd

been struggling to come up with someone for the position. Blake doesn't want the role, in spite of having the skill set for it, and no amount of badgering on our part can convince her otherwise.

"Me?"

Nodding, I wait for him to get his head around what I'm asking.

"You can't possibly think—"

"No. We don't *think*. We *know*."

Shaking his head, he says, "I appreciate the vote of confidence, I do, but I've never coached in my life."

"You've been captain of your team for the last three years, before that you were assistant captain for four. You spend every off season helping with numerous clinics the country over. You've been instrumental in leading whatever team you've played on to finals and championships over the years." I cock my head and raise an eyebrow. "Should I go on?"

"No. I know what I've done. Your knowledge surprises me though. You don't strike me as a hockey fan."

"I'm more than a fan. One of my best friends comes from a family who could arguably be called hockey royalty and has played in three Olympics. Two gold medals, one silver."

"Okay, so you might know a bit about the game but how much do you know about owning a team and not just owning it, *building* it. You're starting from scratch. The ground up."

"Which is why I'm setting those foundations with solid footings. And you, Walker Alcott, are my head coach. You're the man I believe, the Rogues GM and assistant coach believe, will ground the team and use your considerable skills and knowledge to lead us to the finals our first year in the league."

"The finals? Jesus fuck, woman, you're asking a lot. The impossible."

"Here's where I tell you I love a good challenge. It's why I'm offering you a bonus for the first year we play. You get us to the finals, and I'll pay you double your salary. I've already written the check."

"I haven't said yes to the job."

"I'm confident you will."

"How can you be? I've got no record. No experience."

"You don't need on-job experience for this. You love the game, live and breathe it, you have the drive to succeed and the determination and dedication to get where you want, *what* you want. And, right now you need a new focus. Something where you can capitalize on the years you've devoted to hockey."

"I know how to play."

"Don't sell yourself short. To play at your level, to succeed the way you have, you have to know the game inside and out. Every angle of it. On and off the ice. You and Blake are going to make a formidable coaching team."

"Blake?"

"Your assistant coach. Blake Watts."

"Blake *Watts*? How the hell did you get her? Last I heard she was coaching the Canadian women's hockey team."

I grin. "That best friend I referred to? That would be Blake."

"Jesus. You're right, the Watts family are hockey royalty. Fuck, the woman's more qualified for head coach than I am. She coached the Canadians to Olympic gold, for fuck's sake."

"She doesn't want the head coach job. And full disclosure, which you'll get more of before you sign your contract, she's also one quarter of KAW."

"Shit. She co-owns the team?"

"Indirectly, yes. Or not. KAW owns the Rogues franchise and Blake, myself, and two others own KAW."

"Isn't it a conflict of interest for her to be employed by the team?"

"No. KAW is privately owned. The only people we answer to are ourselves. The Rogues GM is also a co-owner of KAW."

"Are you all going to work for the team?"

"No. Our fourth partner has no interest in sport outside of supporting her friend play. And with Blake no longer playing, I don't expect her interest in the game to change."

"Another woman? Four women? The Rogues are owned by women?" Walker laughs and laughs hard. "Oh god, this is going to be one hell of a battle."

My back jerks straight. "Do you have an issue with women in positions of power, Mr. Alcott?" From everything I've read about him, I didn't think he did but maybe I'm wrong.

"Hell no. I'm going to cheer you on. Okay, if I say yes, what's the plan from here? When does the team start in the league? Where are the team facilities? When do you start picking players?"

"Lots of questions and I'm sure you'll have more. But before we get to those, I have one for you."

"Shoot."

"When can you start?"

"I." Walker snaps his mouth shut. "I haven't said yes."

"But you're going to."

"I love your confidence. I wish I had it."

"You will." Deciding to give him time to digest what's on offer, I say, "Why don't I get Tanya back in here so we can finish the photo shoot. Then when we're done, we'll head to my hotel where we can talk about my plans for the Rogues and you, more."

"You still want me to be the face of Rogue's new athletic pants?"

"Why wouldn't I?"

"Well, you know, the whole, no pants thing."

I laugh. "Walker, if you think any woman is going to take offense to you dropping your pants, you're insane. Besides, what you got going on is definitely worth taking a look at."

He ducks his head, but I still see the flush of red slash across his cheeks. "I apologize. It's not something I would normally do."

"Walker, you have one of the cleanest reps in the league. Aside from the whole practice-wife thing. I trust you to represent Rogue sportswear and the Rogues hockey team with propriety and respect."

"You can't know that. Especially after what you walked in on."

"I can." I push to my feet, preparing to go in search of Tanya. "Remember that PI? Kristina Bancroft isn't the only person I had him investigate."

I leave him to think about that while I go to find Tanya. She's probably in her office, which is where I left the bags of merchandise I want Walker to model.

I'd been so pissed when my car had gotten caught in traffic and I knew I'd be late. I had planned time to talk to Walker before the shoot.

I smile at the memory of Walker dropping his pants, the cocky smirk on his face forced until Tanya had all but swallowed her tongue and his smile turned genuine.

If I'd known what I'd walk in on when I finally got here, I wouldn't have wasted the energy on anger and frustration.

Speaking of frustration.

I haven't been sexually attracted to a man in months. I can't even remember the last time I had sex. Maybe last year? The reality is I've had far more exciting things going on in my life.

And this morning was the reward for months, hell years, of hard work and planning, of out maneuvering and playing the old-boy network that believes professional hockey is a men-only world.

Today, as the CEO of KAW, I signed a deal with the National Hockey League that will bring, not only a national professional sport, but much needed jobs and community to my beloved hometown.

It has been a hard road so far and I have no doubt it will only get harder.

Once word gets out about the franchise details, I expect backlash. From where the team will be located, to the people running the organization, to the employees, I fully expect to have to defend every choice, every decision.

But it doesn't matter. It will be more than worth it when we hit the end of our first season as winners.

I have no plans to allow this team to fail. I'll make sure they have everything they need to succeed.

By the time we take to the ice the first time, the players, coaching staff, supporting staff, the front office, all their families, will be one big family, a community set on one goal and one goal only.

Winning.

Finding Tanya where I expect, I grab the bags of Rogue merchandise and say, "I'll head out and get Walker in the first of what I want photographed."

"Ah, is he…"

I laugh at Tanya's flustered response. "Yes. He's covered."

"Oh."

I can't tell if she's happy about that or not. I also can't decide if I'm upset by the thought of her being disappointed she won't see him half naked again.

That's something I'll have to ponder later. Right now, I want to get this shoot over with so Walker and I can head to my hotel and hash out the rest of the details so we can get his contract altered if needed and his signature on the bottom of it.

I have no doubt he'll sign.

The man needs us as much as we need him, and I plan to make sure we both get exactly what we need.

Time slips away as we get through all the gear I want to take photos of Walker wearing. He's a feast for the eyes, clothed or not, and regardless of his recent injury and shift from elite athlete to elite athlete coach, he has the body to make our sportswear look good.

And who says you have to be a professional athlete to wear our clothes?

No one. This new line might be in our high performance collection designed for elite athletes but Rogue has collections of clothing for the everyday man—or woman—too.

Our women's line is what started the business. It's what we've built our empire on. It's our foundation. And it's given us the ability to see our dreams come true.

Walker is in the final outfit, a pair of ankle length compression pants and a matching long sleeve shirt. He might be clothed from neck to ankle but there is nothing left to the imagination here.

Every inch of him is on display.

Every mound of muscle, every dip of manly flesh is right there. I know these particular garments are meant to be worn beneath other clothes but damn, I'm going to have to have a word with the girls.

The designers can't know how revealing this design is. The material is so thin, so tight, Walker may as well be wearing paint, and as he heats up under the studio lights, the fabric seems to reveal more.

I kept this set for last because I knew he'd sweat in them and while there's nothing wrong with seeing our clothing hard at work, I didn't want to leave him sticky and uncomfortable the whole time Tanya directed him and moved around, her camera clicking.

"Can you drop your chin to your chest, put your hands on your hips like you've just completed a..." Tanya looks over the top of her camera. "A workout?"

Walker's laughter floats around us. "You're not into exercise, are you?" he asks Tanya.

"Does walking to the bathroom count?" she asks while putting her eye back to her camera.

Her answer has us all laughing. And in spite of Walker not being in the position she asked, Tanya clicks away, capturing what I'm sure are going to be the best shots of this whole session.

He's gorgeous. There's no denying it, but right now, with pure joy radiating off him, he's spectacular. "We're going to use those."

Tanya glances at me over her shoulder, the grin on her face saying it all. She sees what I see.

"But take the ones you wanted too." I remind them both of

her directions and watch as Walker seamlessly morphs from carefree pleasure to serious just-finished-a-grueling-workout pose.

If I didn't want the man to coach my team, I'd be seriously trying to talk him into a career in modeling. Hell, I might even make him the permanent face of Rogue.

Both clothing line and team.

Pondering that, I wait for Tanya to call the shoot.

Once she's let Walker go change, I head over to her. "I want copies of those laughing shots sent to my personal email."

"What's swirling in that head of yours?" she asks.

"Not sure yet."

"Oh, you're sure. I've known you long enough to know when you're being hit by a brilliant idea."

"You have known me a while."

"Don't say how long." She holds up a hand. "Neither of us needs to be reminded of how old we are," she adds with a chuckle.

"True."

We're interrupted when Walker comes back. "Do you still want to talk?" His words are muffled by the shirt he's pulling over his head.

I've spent the last few hours seeing him in various stages of undress and yet that one move, the simple donning of a t-shirt, has my insides tightening and my heart rate picking up speed.

I'm not sure how I feel about this attraction. I'm not going to lie to myself. I want him.

For the team.

For me.

Except I don't mix business and pleasure.

Then again, I've never been tempted the way I am with Walker.

The next few months are going to be interesting. With the backlash I'm sure to get from the franchise announcement to the sexual tension zinging between us, the road to that first game is going to be a challenge.

But like I told Walker earlier.

I love a challenge.

WALKER

I scrub a hand over my face, the stubble on my jaw rasping against my palm.

I'm exhausted.

And this stupid meeting isn't helping.

Jerry Cantrell sits across from me, a smug look on his face.

He wouldn't look so pleased if he knew what I had on him.

I still haven't decided what to do about the pictures yet.

Oh, I know I'm going to use them to get Kristina out of my life completely. Just the threat of making them public would guarantee that. The woman is all about her image. Always has been.

So many red flags flapping.

From the first night I met her and she made her interest clear, I should have seen them.

Seen *her*.

"You good with that then?" Drake asks.

"We're good with that," Jerry replies.

"Sir—"

"I said, we're good." Jerry glares at the woman beside him. Mischa is the PR VP for the New York Knights and I know she's not happy Jerry doesn't want the team to make a joint announcement of my retirement.

"Then we'll leave you to get on with your day." Drake collects the papers in front of him. The drafts of my announcement. "Thanks for meeting with us on short notice."

I can tell Drake is only being polite; he's made it clear over the last few years how little he respects Jerry. And I'd be lying if I said I didn't fall in with Drake's assessment of the man who owns the team I'm no longer contracted to.

My time with New York is done.

The lawyers will do their thing, and there will be paperwork to sign I'm sure, but as of now I'm not on the roaster.

I'm not a player.

I'm not anything.

But I could be.

I still have to meet Oakley.

We'd planned to head to her hotel the minute we'd finished the shoot, but I knew I couldn't put Drake off any longer and when I'd made that call, he'd insisted we meet with the team immediately.

So here we are, three hours later, no better off than before we arrived.

We could have dealt with this over the phone. But I get why Drake wanted to do it in person. He doesn't want me to burn bridges and even though I can't tell him about Oakley's offer, I know if he knew, he'd remind me of the necessity to stay on amicable terms with my old team.

Pushing to my feet, I lean over the table and offer my hand. "It's been a pleasure playing for the New York Knights. I'm sorry we had to end our association this way."

"I'm sorry you missed out on the Cup." Jerry doesn't stand, just reaches out and puts his hand in mine. His grip is weak, his hand limp, and I'm reminded of how this man didn't get where he is because of hard work.

Gerald Cantrell Senior is the reason the team has been a success and why Jerry Junior now owns it.

"I've got two already, although I am sorry we never made it there together." It's lip service. I don't mean any of it.

Yes, I'm sad we haven't won the Cup as a team since he took over two years ago but I'm not sorry Jerry doesn't have that privilege. The cups the Knights have brought home were all under Gerald Senior's reign.

"We'll deal with the team's lawyers from now on. No need to interrupt your day again," Drake says as his hand replaces mine in Jerry's. "Again, thanks for seeing us on short notice."

Jerry pulls his hand from Drake's and pushes his ample weight out of his chair. "I've got another meeting to get to. Good luck with whatever you do next, Alcott." Showing me Drake and I aren't the only ones saying things out of fake politeness, his back is turned and he's striding from the room before I can reply.

Not that I was going to comment. I've never been a fan and after the photos Oakley gave me, I'm even less of one. I'm glad I won't be around when that shit gets made public because if I've learned anything about Kristina over the last few years, it's she does everything for a reason. And that reason is to climb a ladder.

It might have taken me a while—and Oakley shoving those photos in my face—but I finally see the woman for who she is. And Jerry Cantrell might think he's in control of their little affair, but I'd bet the money I earned on my contract with Rogue sportswear she's going to blow up his world.

"Walker, if you don't mind, can I get a copy of your media announcement so I can draft a statement from the team?" Mischa asks.

"Sure. Although I thought Jerry didn't want to make the announcement."

"He doesn't and we won't, but we will need to make a comment on yours."

"Ah, yeah, sorry, I wasn't thinking." I glance at the door Jerry went through. "Is it going to be an issue for you?"

She shakes her head and smiles. "No. He might think he runs the place, but Rafe will be extremely vocal about the results of this meeting. He'll want to be sure you leaving the team is handled correctly."

I nod. Neither of us voicing that we both think Jerry is not handling this the right way. Rafe would be here if it weren't for his kid being in hospital. "I hope Rafe's son is okay."

"I'm sure he will be. He's not the first nine-year-old to break an arm."

"No. Guess not. Okay, well, let Rafe know he can give me a call if he wants." I don't know what we would talk about at this point except I consider New York's GM a friend as well as my boss and I definitely don't want to leave here without thanking him for all he's done for me over the years.

Although, I'm not sure I should speak to him if I take Oakley up on her offer.

"C'mon, we can stop at your lawyer's office before we head back to mine." Drake grabs his briefcase.

"Can't it wait until tomorrow?" I want to get to Oakley. I'm not ready to say yes—I still need some questions answered—but I've always followed my gut, and my gut tells me to go to Oakley.

Whether that's because of her offer or the sizzle of attraction between us, I'm not sure. And at this point I don't care.

I want to see her again.

Now.

In fact, that's exactly what I'm going to do. "I need to do something. I'll meet you at your office first thing in the morning." I clap Drake on the back. "You don't need me to talk to my lawyer, I trust you to do what's necessary. I'll sign anything I need to tomorrow."

What I don't add is that I might have something else for him to look at.

Do coaches need agents?

It's something I've never thought about. I'll need a lawyer at least, to look over any contract Oakley gives me.

"We need to get the press release finalized and distributed."

"Tomorrow."

"But—"

I give him the one thing I know he won't argue against. "I need to speak to Shelby."

Drake knows my sister is everything to me. I became her guardian after our parents died and while she'd been a few months from going off to college and anything but a kid at the time, I was still responsible for her. Any offer Drake gets for me or comes across his desk is vetted with Shelby in mind.

"You haven't told her?"

Shaking my head, I say, "No, not yet. I want to tell her in person, before it goes public."

"Sure. Sure. Get going then. I'll see you in the morning."

Leaving Drake with Mischa, I stride from the conference room, head high, gaze straight ahead. I don't want to make eye contact. The last thing I need is to have to lie to someone about why I'm here. I'd rather tell the team in person, or maybe I'll send out a group text after I speak with Shelby.

Tomorrow.

Today I'm going to spend time with a woman who might just be my salvation.

My injury might have ended my dream, but it also might have given me a life.

I'm the first to admit I haven't really thought about what I'd do when my playing career was over. Oakley stumped me earlier because what I told her was true.

I believed I'd play into my late thirties.

I'm twenty-nine in a month.

Ten years ahead of my plan.

Not that I'd really had a plan. Play, train, rinse, repeat—that's the extent of my plan.

I blew more than my knees all those months ago. I scrambled my brain and blew up my life.

Or what there was of it.

Shit. My personal life was already in the toilet when I took that hit and that fiasco had only gotten worse.

Kristina had already been in my rearview mirror, not that she'd accepted we were over, and that's when the real drama with her started. If I wasn't already down, I'd kick myself for ever falling for her.

Then again, the only time I thought deeply about our relationship was when she brought it up.

I never thought about her when we weren't together. Not like I did once I'd broken up with her and she wouldn't leave me the hell alone, and none of those thoughts were with affection.

I've known Oakley James a grand total of seven hours and I've thought more about her than any other woman beside my sister.

Is it because I want to fuck her?

Or is it the lifeline she's offering me with this new franchise?

Either would be fine. Except, I have a feeling it's both.

How that will play out is yet to be determined. I still haven't made my decision about the job...

And yet, I'm heading for her hotel to talk about it.

There isn't really anything else to discuss. She gave me the bare bones of the deal. I just need to give her an answer.

Am I ready to do that? Or am I hoping I'll get to shuck my pants in front of her again?

I need to work out what I'm doing before I see her.

I'm either heading to her hotel to talk about the Rogues or to strip her naked and fuck her against the nearest flat surface.

It amazes me that both those scenarios have an equal level of excitement fizzing through my veins.

Especially when sex hasn't been on my mind at all in over a year.

One look at Oakley James and I'm a drooling Neanderthal unable to think about anything but my base needs.

Exiting the team offices, I pause on the sidewalk and look up.

The sky is still blue and still above my head.

It didn't crash down on me when I told Jerry I was retiring. I'd fully expected to be crushed by the weight of that decision. Of saying it out loud to someone other than Drake and making it official.

Instead, my heart is thumping with anticipation of seeing Oakley. My steps are light and the only thing I feel leaving the building behind me is relief.

For the last six months my life has been ruled by doctors and tests and scans and the prospect of my career being over. Right now, I don't have the suffocating feeling that has been my constant since my knees slammed into the boards and my head snapped against the glass.

I feel...

Free.

It's the only word I can think of. The outcome of my injuries might not be one I want but the results are what they are and now I'm free to move on to what's next.

Is it being head coach of the Baton Rouge Rogues?

Is that what I want?

I don't know. Except I can't deny the thrill that floods my veins. The anticipation of starting a team from scratch. Of guiding them and pushing them to be their best. Of building them up and making them champions.

Oakley wants to make the finals our first year in the league. With the right players, it could be done. I'm not going to delude myself into thinking we can get the pick of the league—I know we can't, but what we can do is pick the best available and mold them, pull them together and turn them into a game-winning team.

I want that.

Holy fucking shit.

I want that!

And right here, on the sidewalk outside the New York Knights' front office, I've made my decision. I'm searching the street, striding to the curb, my arm raised to flag a cab before I've even finished that thought.

In seconds I'm in the back seat giving the cabbie the name of Oakley's hotel and grinning like a fool.

The sensations racing through me are ones I've only found one other place. On the ice.

Yeah, it's not what I pictured myself doing and if I'm honest I wouldn't be if I had a choice, but I'm doing it.

I *want* to do it.

I'm going to be the head coach of the National Hockey League's newest franchise, the Baton Rouge Rogues.

I'm going Rogue.

The Rogue sportswear slogan pops into my head.

Go your own way. Go Rogue.

I'm doing that. I'm going rogue.

I'm still grinning like an idiot when I toss money at the cab driver before he even comes to a complete stop in front of Oakley's hotel.

My smile outshines the one on the bellboy's face when he opens my door. I even toss him a twenty as I stride past, not slowing my pace as I head inside.

I can't get to the elevators fast enough.

I know where I'm going. Oakley gave me her room number before we parted earlier.

Now all I have to do is get upstairs and give her my answer.

I don't take in the opulent foyer or the exotic flowers in vases on pedestals. I'm single focused, my goal in sight. Reaching the elevator alcove, I stab the up button hard. Twice. I'm itching to get up there and tell her what I've decided.

I'm trying not to think about what this means. That I'll have to leave New York. Leave Shelby. We haven't lived in a different city since our parents died. And I'm probably worrying over nothing—she's not a kid now.

Fuck, as of last month, she's not even a college student anymore.

A niggle of worry tugs. She'll be looking for her own apartment soon. I want her to move back into my place and maybe now I won't be here, she will. I can keep the apartment for her. I'll buy something when I relocate. Or lease something. Whatever. None of that matters right now.

What matters is telling Oakley yes.

The elevator opens and I step in, move to the back as more people board. By the time the doors close again, the damn thing is full, and as it rises to the top I grit my teeth at every stop it makes, tap my fists against my thighs in an agitated rhythm.

I barely notice the people around me although I hear the whispers, my name; I know I'm recognized.

All I can think is *please don't talk to me*. The last thing I want to do is sign autographs or take selfies.

Thankfully I'm left alone and I'm the last passenger when the doors open on the top floor. I'm out and down the hall to Oakley's door, my fist banging on it within seconds.

When the door opens, I'm greeted by a towel-wrapped Oakley, her hair in some kind of messy knot on top of her head that shouldn't be sexy but is, and for a moment my brain freezes.

My gaze goes from those chaotic strands of auburn hair to her perfectly polished pink toenails and I'm sporting my second instant erection of the day.

This woman.

She gets to me in a way I've never experienced, and I'll be fucked if I want to do anything about it other than drop my pants for her again.

I step forward.

She steps back.

Again, I take a step and so does she.

Our breaths are labored, and I'm sure my eyes are as dilated as hers, and her heart has to be racing as fast as mine.

I can't think of anything except touching her. Getting inside her. I want her all over me. I want to be all over her.

But my brain isn't functioning right, and I can't seem to string the right words together.

I'm in her suite, shutting the door behind me with a hard shove, and the only thing I can do is blurt out one word.

"Yes."

OAKLEY

"Yes!"

That one word echoes around me and it takes a few seconds for me to say or do anything because I don't know what Walker is saying yes to.

Is he talking about coaching the Rogues?

Hope flutters in my chest.

Or is he talking about doing something with the crackling chemistry that arcs between us?

The fluttering from that thought takes place lower down and I'm left in a struggle of indecision.

Which answer do I want?

Right now, with my skin on fire and my sex clenching tight, I know which I want him to be saying yes to. Except I want both, and really, we should be able to have both, right?

We're adults, unattached and free to fuck whoever we want.

And right now, in this moment, I want to fuck Walker Alcott more than I want him to coach the Rogues.

Which tells me we're going to have to figure out how to work together while sharing a bed because just looking at him, I know once won't be enough.

Fisting the knot of my towel I step forward, the first step I've taken toward him since he arrived. A quick yank and my towel drops to the floor, and I'm grinning when I say, "It seems only fair I show you mine after you showed me yours."

The laugh that erupts from Walker is short and sharp and in the next second it's cut off by my mouth on his.

I don't remember moving. Maybe it was him, maybe it's his mouth crashing onto mine.

Doesn't matter, the wet heat of our mouths plastered together, the sweep of his tongue on mine, the press of my naked body to his clothed one are the only important things.

My back hits something hard, pushing a burst of air from my lungs. Walker swallows the gasp, his mouth devouring mine with a greed I've never experienced.

He's good, better than good, but it doesn't feel practiced or new. It's like our mouths have been kissing for years and this dance is one we know well.

One that's as natural to us as breathing.

"Bed." Walker pants into my mouth. "Where's the bed?"

"Too far." My hands scrabble at his shirt, pushing it up to dive beneath so I can get my fingers on hard, hot flesh. "The floor."

He jerks back, his mouth leaving mine, and stares at me with fire in his eyes before he nods and takes us to the floor.

The timber is cool against my skin and goose bumps explode from head to toe. I shiver from the chill but in the few seconds I've stretched out on the floor Walker has stripped himself bare and the heat of him blankets me.

I take his weight; it's a comforting crush I want—need—and when his cock presses against my slick flesh I'm helpless to hold in the moan of pleasure that escapes me.

He's hot and throbbing, and instinct has me parting my legs so his length can slip deeper.

Rocking my hips, I rub my clit against his shaft, and with his tongue tangled with mine I race straight up and over the first peak. I buck and shudder, riding the high with a strangled cry.

Walker curses, fumbles around, then shoves a hand between

us. His knuckles brush my swollen clit, sending pulses of pleasure shooting into my core so sharp I lose my breath.

I haven't come down; it's not as intense, but the spasms continue to clench my pussy, and without thought or instruction I lift my legs and wrap them around his waist, crossing my ankles near his shoulder blades. I grip the back of my knees and hold them tight.

I'm almost folded in half, and I thank years of yoga for my flexibility.

"Fuck." Walker leans back, his eyes darting from side to side. "I want to look but I can't wait."

His words don't make sense until he lines the tip of his cock to my soaked entrance and drives deep in one sense-jarring thrust.

The cry that bursts from my throat is raw and needy, and my fingers claw the back of my legs, my nails digging in.

"Want you with me," Walker mutters. "Hands up above your head."

"But—"

"I've got them."

And he has. He slips his arms beneath my calves, his upper arms pressing against the back of my thighs to hold my legs in place, and plants his hands on the floor beside my head. Our eyes catch and we're stuck for long seconds.

So much is said in that one look. It's clear as a sunny day. Neither of us will be satisfied with just tonight.

I've never connected with a man the way I am with Walker. I don't know him and yet...

I do.

It should scare me but doesn't. I've never backed down from anything, and whatever this is with Walker we'll work through it, see where it leads, because even though neither of us has said a word, we're communicating.

I see his acknowledgment, his determination.

We're in this together.

In silent agreement he moves.

A slow drag out, a quick thrust in.

I'm strong but I don't have leverage to move with him. I'm caught and totally at his mercy and the thrill that shoots through me steals my breath.

I've never ceded control like this. Not in any aspect of my life. Especially not in a physical relationship. It's the most vulnerable place a woman can be, and I've always protected myself.

And yet with Walker I'm opening up and giving him everything. I feel it. Both physically and emotionally.

This isn't a comfortable thought, and yet it feels right to give myself to him.

"You with me?" he growls.

I nod. I'm trapped, held tight between him and the floor. I don't have the breath to talk but my eyes speak for me because in the next instant he stops, and his hands find their way to frame my face, his gaze boring into mine.

"No. You're not."

Before I can protest, he lifts up, pulls free of my clenching pussy, and jumps to his feet.

I have no idea how he manages the move so fast and lowers my legs gently at the same time. I don't know if he's stopping or if he's changing positions or—

"Stop." He reaches down and scoops me up. One arm behind my knees, the other my back, and then I'm in his arms, against his chest, and he's heading deeper into the suite. "Which room?"

I point to the one on the right. The other is empty, I haven't even been in there. Nat was supposed to come to New York with me, to be there when I signed the agreement on behalf of KAW with the National Hockey League, but at the last minute we decided to keep her out of it for now.

"You're still not with me," Walker murmurs as we enter the bedroom I'm using.

"I'm sorry."

"Don't be." He smiles down at me. "We kind of rushed into this."

"Yeah."

"I don't regret anything other than taking you like an animal on the floor."

"Oh. You—"

"Don't get me wrong. Hot hard sex the second we get behind a closed door has its place but not the first time." He lowers me to the bed, then cages me in with a hand either side of my head. Locking his gaze with mine he says, "The first time I come inside you, you'll be with me."

I can't decide it that's a promise or a threat. His voice holds an edge, one I feel vibrating through every cell. Should I agree? Give him permission to do what he wants? I've never been this unsure about anything in my life. Not since my grandfather rescued me from my—*no*—I'm not going there.

"You're doing it again."

My focus comes back to the man leaning over me. "Sorry?"

"You keep disappearing." He taps my temple. "In here."

"Oh. Sorry."

Walker grins. "Remember telling me you like a challenge?" I nod. "Well, so do I, and I think you're going to be my biggest challenge. Possibly my greatest reward too."

The last sentence is murmured and the words, what they imply, rock me. I know this thing between us is different. I want to say it has to do with the excitement of getting the franchise, but I know that's a lie, and one thing I've always refused to do is lie to myself.

It's Walker.

It's me and Walker.

Us together.

"Oak." His face comes closer. "Stop thinking so hard. You need to relax."

A shiver rolls over me when he brushes his nose along my jaw and the breath he sucks in, the fact he presses closer, breathes deeper...

"*Walker.*"

"Yeah, I know."

What does he know? I don't understand anything right now.

"Lie back and let me have you." His gaze is back on mine, and I know he's asking for more than my body.

Swallowing, I lick my lips, roll them between my teeth. Instinct tells me to give him everything. Except I'm so used to keeping myself back, being the one in control, that it's hard to let him any deeper than surface level.

"How about this?" He straightens up, his gaze moving over me like a physical caress. "You let me have my way with this gorgeous body tonight, and we'll worry about everything else later."

I understand what he's doing. He's making this physical, attempting to remove the emotions to take away the concern he must see. I've never had a problem hiding my feelings before. I'm pretty sure I didn't have a problem earlier today.

Except now we're both naked. Behind closed doors with no chance of anyone interrupting us.

"Oak." I focus my eyes on his. "We can stop."

"No!" I'm up, my arms around his neck before I finish the word. The action tells me all I need to know. I'm an instinctual person; yes, I use my intellect too, but the best decisions of my life have been made because my instincts have told me to make them. "I don't want to stop."

"Then we won't." He lowers his face to the curve of my neck and presses a kiss there before asking, "Were you getting in, already in, or getting out of the shower when I got here?"

"Getting in."

His head lifts and his eyes bore into mine. With a sexy tilt of his lips, he asks, "Want me to wash your back?"

I tip my head to the side, contemplating his question. Do I want to shower with him? I've always found showering and sleeping with a man far more intimate than sex. It's a line I've rarely crossed and yet I find myself wanting to cross it with Walker.

Hell, I'm thinking of grabbing his hand and racing to the bathroom.

"Oakley," he murmurs. "I'm going to be honest with you. I don't normally do this. I'm not one to jump into bed with a woman the day I meet her but with you..." His gaze searches mine.

Nodding I say, "I know."

"I have no idea what this is, where it will go, what it will mean to our working relationship, and considering you're going to be my boss we probably shouldn't—"

I press my hand to his mouth. "I'm not going to be your direct boss."

"Does that really make a difference?" he asks against my hand.

With a shrug I give him a truth I feel to my bones. "I don't really care."

I feel one side of his mouth kick up beneath my fingers. "You don't care?"

Removing my hand, I move back, leaning into the arms he has wrapped around me. "I care. What I'm saying is I think whatever this is, because like you, I have no idea what it is, I think it's worth the risk our professional positions pose."

Walker nods. "So we do this then—"

"Wait!" I palm both sides of his face. "I just realized what you said. You're taking the job!"

His face softens, a smile spreading his lips. "You knew I would."

"Yeah, I did."

"There's a lot we need to go over."

"You want to do it now?" I don't know about him, but I'm more than happy to forget everything outside of this room and the two of us until tomorrow.

"We probably should."

"But do you want to?" I move closer, my lips almost brushing his. "Or do you want to wash my back?"

I'm off the bed, held tight to Walker's body and heading for the bathroom in answer.

I grin. "Okay, back washing it is."

"It'll be more than that," he growls.

I like that he seems as desperate as me to finish what we started before I let my thoughts stop us.

When Walker makes it into the bathroom, he looks around, taking in the luxurious fittings. His gaze locks on the huge tub in the corner. "As appealing as that multi-head shower looks, I think we're going to take advantage of the tub."

Plopping my naked butt on the counter, he leans in and kisses me. A long, deep, wet kiss that sucks the breath right out of me.

"Don't move," he orders when he's finished scrambling my brain.

He needn't bother. Not when the view of him moving around the room showing me his perfect body, casually pulling off the half-used condom and dropping it in the trash, bending over to start the water and giving me a better look at his ass, has me breathing hard and my fingers twitching to touch.

He's looking through the hotel-supplied toiletries, flicking each one aside when they don't meet his approval, and I can't help but offer assistance. "What are you looking for?"

"Hmm..." he hums absently as he picks up the final bottle. Popping the cap, he takes a sniff before bringing it to me. "Here. Smell good?"

The fact he's asking for my opinion shocks me. It shouldn't. Walker has been considerate up until now. He's a genuinely nice guy. I know that from the file my PI gave me but also from experience. In spite of what he did when we first met, he's not a cocky asshole. And I can't let him put that stuff in the bath. "No. It smells like a flower shop."

"Huh. You don't like flowers..." He eyes me carefully. "Do you not like it for you or me?"

How the hell can he read me so easily? "Ah..."

"Right. Okay. Well, I'm man enough to survive smelling like a flower shop."

"But—"

"Plus you can jump in the shower with me to make sure you wash it all away before we leave in the morning."

Ooo, I like the way he thinks. "I can do that."

"Oh, no, there is no can, you *will* do that." He grins at me, a cocky, I'm going to get you to do exactly what I want grin, that has me smiling in return.

"You sure about that?" I ask, even though we both know I'll do it.

"Absolutely," he says, while dumping a good amount of the sweet smelling liquid from the bottle into the stream of water filling the tub.

"Cocky," I mutter.

Walker looks at me over his shoulder, his eyes locking with mine. "Confident."

I have no come back for that because he should be confident. He had me naked on the floor, his cock buried inside me within minutes of his arrival.

I'm a sure thing.

Except I'm not.

I've never done this with anyone.

I'm cautious, often calculating, when it comes to the men I sleep with.

Usually, it's sex. Only sex.

But with Walker, I knew before I dropped that towel it was more than sex. More than two people giving in to the chemistry sizzling between them.

I don't believe in love at first sight—lust at first sight sure, but love? And I'm not saying that's what this is. Even with the investigation the PI did, I don't *know* Walker.

And yet...

I do.

It's the most discombobulating sensation I've ever felt.

It should be scary, and in some regards it is, but I'm going to embrace it.

Things could blow up in my face—in our faces now that he's agreed to take the head coach job with the Rogues, but like I said earlier...

It will be worth the risk.

We will be worth the risk.

WALKER

If someone told me a week ago I'd be here, in this tub with a gorgeous woman in my arms, I would have laughed in their face.

Hell, if they'd told me a few hours ago, I'd have done the same.

But Oakley is unlike any woman I've ever known.

She's not the first competent, successful women I've met, or the most beautiful for that matter.

Playing a professional sport has had me surrounded by good-looking accomplished women for years. In all that time I've never encountered one who triggered the reaction Oakley does.

It feels like I've known her forever. And yet, there is so much about her I don't know.

I didn't bother Googling her. Don't get me wrong, I was tempted. But then, Oakley tempts me on so many levels.

Personally, professionally.

I want this woman.

I want what she's offering me.

And if I'm honest, since my injury I haven't felt this at ease or pumped up.

Just being with her smooths out the turbulent emotions I've

been dealing with the last few months and excites me in a way I haven't been since we landed in the playoffs last season.

Shit, even last season's success didn't have me thrumming with anticipation the way Oakley's offer does.

"What are you thinking about?"

Her soft voice floats around us almost like it's part of the steam hanging in the air. "You."

"Oh?"

I squeeze her a little tighter. "You're an incredible woman."

"Thank you. But I doubt that's what you were thinking about." She tilts her head back to look at me, the arch of one eyebrow voicing the question her mouth doesn't.

"True." Dropping a quick kiss to her temple, I lean back and reveal more than I probably should. "You settle me. I can't explain it. I just feel as though after months of upheaval, the ground beneath my feet is finally steady."

"It's probably more the job you've accepted than me."

"No. That's part of it, sure, but it's you. And at the risk of diving deeper than either of us will be comfortable with, I have to tell you this—us, together—is the most right thing I've ever felt. And that includes when I strap on skates and hit the ice, and I feel pretty damn right doing that."

"Your injury, the shift in career focus makes that feel less right."

"Again, no. This here, you and me, feels far more right than hockey ever has."

Her body goes taut against me.

Fuck.

I shouldn't have said that.

Except putting that out there also feels right.

I know it's fast, I know we barely know each other even though I've had my dick in her. We're connected on a level I never expected, a depth that should scare the shit out of me, and it does.

There's a healthy dose of fear skating through my veins right alongside the knowledge that I'm meant to be here, with her.

This woman, she has me tied tight. Even with the fear of what's to come, I'm not unhappy.

Less than twenty-four hours ago I would have said nothing could make me happy.

Not a woman.

Not a job offer.

Nothing short of being told I'd play again at the same level I did before Blanchett slammed me into those boards would have made me happy.

Hours.

It's taken a measly few hours for the woman in my arms to change everything about my life.

This morning everything I'd worked for had been ripped out from under me and I had no clear view of where to go next until she walked out from behind those blinding lights and my body went on hyper alert.

I hadn't recognized it then. I should have. I'd never reacted to a woman like that in my life, but I'd put it down to the numbness my relationship with Kristina had left me in.

It took one look at Oakley James for my body to realize I wasn't dead.

It took a bit longer for my brain to catch up.

And while it's too early to talk about my heart, I'm positive it's involved here.

I can't put it into words. Don't want to. Not yet. There are too many things that need to be dealt with first.

But for now, I'm going to enjoy the woman in my arms and this night before either of us has to face the world outside this suite.

Bending my head, I bring my lips to her ear and whisper, "Talk to me."

"This is big."

I hear her hesitation. Her fear. "It is."

"It could get complicated."

"There's no *could* about it. It's going to get complicated as fuck."

Her whole body softens on a deep sigh. "We need a plan."

"A plan?"

"How to handle our relationships."

I'm glad she put the s on the end of that word because if we're going to make either a success, we need to know there is a distinction.

Personal and professional.

A line we both need to be aware of from the start. "I think this one should be easy enough."

"The other would be too. *If* we weren't in this one. It's the two together, the bridge between them that is going to need managing."

"I'll do whatever you think is best as long as that isn't ending either. But if one has to go, I'd prefer it not be us."

I need that out there. I don't know why, except the thought of not being with Oakley cuts deeper than the thought of not coaching her new team. Cuts sharper than walking away from hockey all together.

Sitting up, she spins on her knees to face me. "You'd give up the coaching job for me?"

The surprise and confusion in her voice is matched by the look in her eyes. And I give her the only answer I can. "In a heartbeat."

"Walker." My name is more sigh than word.

Cradling her face in my palms, I bring her closer until our lips almost touch. "I know."

"I never expected this. You."

"Join the club."

"How do we make this work?"

"I don't know. Hell, I don't even know what's going to happen tomorrow when the world finds out I'm retiring. Shit. I haven't even told my sister yet."

"You need to do that before it becomes public knowledge."

"I will. After I leave here tomorrow."

"You're staying the night?"

"That should never have been in question."

"Walker." A small smile tilts my lips when she says my name again. I love the sound of it on her tongue.

"Shh..." I press my mouth to hers hard, then pull back. "Tonight we forget about everything outside of this suite. It's just you and me and hours of alone time. Nothing to worry about but each other."

"We should—"

"The only thing we should do is hop out of this tub and get back to what we were doing before I carried you in here."

Putting action to words, I stand and offer her a hand. Once we're both on our feet, I don't delay in grabbing a towel, wrapping it around her shoulders, and lifting her into my arms.

"Are you going to make a habit of carrying me?"

"I like you in my arms."

"I like being in them, but this can't be good for your knees."

She's right, it probably isn't, but if I no longer plan on hitting the ice in a professional game I don't need to take as much care. And as a non-sportsman, my knees are in great shape. "You don't have to worry about that. It's fine."

"Walker."

Her tone is chastising, and I have to laugh. "Is this what a relationship between us will be like? You telling me what to do?"

"I'm not telling you what to do," she huffs. "I am concerned about you hurting yourself."

Placing her on her feet, I wait until her gaze connects with mine before I tell her a truth only my doctors and I know.

"My knees *are* fine. If I were anything but a professional hockey player, I would have been back to work and normal life months ago."

"But—"

I press a finger to her lips. "The damage is repaired; unfortunately neither are or ever will be at the strength or stability they were before the injuries."

I don't tell her the real reason for my need to retire. She'll find out soon enough.

"I still don't want you to hurt yourself."

The fact Oakley isn't concerned because she wants me to play again is refreshing. For months the only concern has been how long until I could be back on the ice.

"I won't push it that far," I promise.

"How will you know? You could trip because you can't see something on the floor, you could bang into—"

"I promise to take care." I can't believe how close her comment is to the true issue. It's probably the perfect place to tell her but I don't. "I still want to be able to take to the ice, and I will, but you're right, anything could happen and not just when I'm carrying you. I could get bumped on the sidewalk, slip down icy stairs, twist the wrong way, there are so many things that could set me back but I'm not going to live my life like I'm disabled. I'm not. Nowhere near it and you have to trust me to know when I'm pushing it too far."

She puffs out a breath and says, "Fine. You know what you can and can't do."

"Ready for me to show what else I can do?" I ask, stepping into her space. I crowd her back toward the bed.

"Oh, and what *can* you do, Mr. Alcott?"

"Any damn thing I want." I pounce, scooping her up in my arms again and dashing for the bed.

With a laugh, I toss her on the covers still rumpled from earlier. Not giving her time to evade me, not that I think she will, I climb onto the mattress and cage her beneath me.

We don't speak for long moments, just gaze into each other's eyes and communicate in a way I've never done before.

This connection we have would be overwhelming if I thought too deeply about it. But when Oakley skims her hands from my shoulders to my groin, I'm not thinking at all.

I'm diving into the woman beneath me with a soul shattering kiss.

I touch her nowhere else; I want her like this.

Mouth to mouth, breath to breath.

I want to savor this contact before moving on to the next. Except Oakley has other ideas, and the hand she wraps around my cock makes it clear what they are.

"Slow," I murmur. "I want to go slow. Take my time getting to know every inch of you."

"We can go slow next time." Her fingers tighten on my shaft. "We've got all night."

I grin against her mouth. "We do. But—"

She shoves her tongue almost down my throat before she pulls back with a nip to my bottom lip and a laugh. "Who knew it would be so easy to shut you up?"

Soothing the sting with the stroke of my tongue, I study her. "You like the idea of being able to shut me up?"

"Hmm..." Her hum is accompanied by a harder pull of her hand along my cock, and I can't stop myself from groaning, from rocking my hips and shoving my dick through her fingers faster. "Nothing else to say, Mr. Alcott?"

I smash the grin on her lips with my own. If she wants us to stop talking, we'll stop. And if she wants things to go fast this round, I'll oblige her. It's not like it would be a sacrifice to take her hard and fast.

Fuck.

I did the minute I stepped into her suite.

We might not have sealed that deal, but we will now. And tomorrow we'll worry about the other deal we're going to seal.

For now, I want to get back between her thighs and sink deep. But when my hard flesh presses into her soft slick sex, I'm struck with a thought no man wants when he's about to be balls deep in the woman he wants more than his next breath.

"Fuck!" I gasp against her lips. "I don't have—"

"What?" Her teeth nip my lip. "What don't you have?"

"Condom. I used the one from my wallet." Another thought hits me. "Shit. I have no idea how old that thing was. It could be out of date. I haven't had a need for over a year."

"We're good. I'm covered. And I'm sure we're both clean."

My gaze meets hers. "Yes. I had every test under the sun when I was hurt."

"Then we're good to go."

Her words slam into me. "But—"

"IUD." She brings her hands up to cup my jaw. "I trust you."

"Are you sure?" I'm not about to push this if she's not. "We can wait."

"The hell we can!"

Using some ninja move too fast for me to see, Oakley has our positions reversed before I take my next breath.

Staring down at me she says, "I trust you."

"You can. But I don't want..." I swallow hard. "Oakley," I breathe out.

"We're doing this. We're going to be together and we're going to do it while we show the world the Rogues are a force to be reckoned with."

Before I can agree or disagree, she lifts up, one hand holding my dick still, the other on my chest. With her eyes on mine, she lowers her body until the tip of me is barely inside her.

"I trust you, Walker."

Her words are like a fist around my heart, squeezing tight, holding on as though nothing could ever pull us apart.

And as she takes me in, a slow slide of her slick flesh down my hard length, I know she means more than the fact we're having sex with nothing between us.

I've never been inside a woman bare. Never thought about it. In fact, I've turned sex down when a condom wasn't available. I like that it's Oakley I'm popping this particular cherry with.

I can't help the smile that stretches my lips or the chuckle that rumbles in my chest.

"Something funny?"

"Yeah."

She stops with an inch or two left to take and for a second I panic. Thinking she's preparing to rise up, I slam my hands on her hips, shove her the rest of the way down. The puff of air that leaves her throat matches the one I suck in at the sensation of being fully inside her.

"Sorry. I was thinking about you taking my cherry."

Blinking at me, her expression is full of confusion, and I laugh again.

"I've never taken a woman bare," I say before she can take offense.

"Oh." Then she's smiling at me. Big and bright and I can't stop myself from sitting up and pressing my mouth to hers.

The kiss is slow and soft and sweet, and I want to keep doing it for hours, but Oakley has other ideas. Hands on my face, she pulls away and locks her gaze on mine.

"I've never let anyone take me bare."

Her confession has my heart tripping in my chest. My blood rushing in my veins. My dick throbbing deep inside her.

Every step of the way we seem to stumble into emotions neither of us are ready for or expecting.

I know what this is, where it's going. I can see it all laid out like a movie reel in my head.

I'm going to grow old with this woman. No matter what happens with the Rogues, if we manage to handle me being head coach or not, I'll be beside Oakley for the rest of my life.

And right now, I want to show her how I'm feeling, because Lord knows we aren't ready for the words.

For me to say them.

Or for her to hear them.

But I can definitely show her. Speak to her heart in a language as old as time.

Lying back, I take her with me and roll. Cradling her face in my hands, I drop my mouth to hers and take her mouth the way I intend to take her body.

Slow and sweet and gentle, I rock us.

With each thrust, I push a little deeper, a little harder but not faster.

It's a languid sweep of our senses, an easy stroll to the peak, and when we finally reach the point of no return with our eyes locked, mouths joined, my cock deep inside her clutching depths, we fly together.

OAKLEY

Before I open my eyes, I have a smile on my face.

Yesterday had been the best day.

And I'm not just smiling about KAW securing the National Hockey League's newest franchise.

No.

The smile on my face has as much to do with the man currently curled around me as reaching a goal we've been working years to attain.

I'm not normally a smug person but I feel pretty damn smug about the Rogues right now. Especially when we were told more than once KAW and the Baton Rouge Rogues wouldn't get the green light.

Walker's fingers flex against my stomach before pressing hard for a fraction of a second then trailing over my skin in tiny circles.

"Morning." His voice rumbles along my neck and against my spine where his chest presses into me. "Regrets?"

A bark of laughter leaves my throat before I can answer him. "Hell no. You?"

"Not on your life."

The hand on my stomach moves upward. His fingers spreading wide, palm flat, he continues until he curls his fingers around my jaw. With a gentle tug, he tilts my head until I can feel his breath on my lips.

Opening my eyes, my gaze meets Walker's sleepy one. His eyes are more gray than blue this morning and I wonder if they change with his moods or the light.

"What are you thinking about?" he asks.

"Your eyes."

"My eyes?" He smiles. "What about them?"

"They're more gray today. Last night they were more blue. Yesterday at the studio they were a mix."

"Yeah, they change depending on the light."

"Not with your mood?"

He shrugs. "Don't know. It's not something I've thought about. Except when someone points it out."

"Hmm..." Maybe we can do an experiment. Arching my back, I press my ass into his groin, wiggle a little to get his attention...

And there. The blue is bleeding in. It's fascinating to watch.

"What are you doing?" he growls with a thrust of his hips.

I grin. "They change with your mood too."

He stills. Pops up on his elbow and leans over me. "You did that on purpose to find that out?"

I'm trying not to laugh at his fake affronted look. But then he pokes me in the side and I'm helpless to stop the laughter from breaking free.

"Oh, it's funny to play with me, is it?" He's up on his hands and knees and flipping me to my back in a second. "Let's see how you like it when I play with you."

I'm laughing harder and enjoying every second of this man's play. This is a side of him I haven't seen yet and I like it.

When I finally manage to get some words out, it's, "You can play with me whenever you want."

It's his turn to laugh when I attempt an eyebrow waggle that I'm sure looks like a demented clown's. Using his distraction, I use the same move I did last night and switch our positions.

"You didn't let me finish what I was doing last night," I say, staring down at him.

His hands find my waist. "You want to be on top?"

"Yes." It's my usual MO. And even though I've let Walker take the lead so far, and enjoyed it, I can't stifle the habits of a lifetime.

"Oakley!" he snaps out my name, bringing me back to the moment. He's eyeing me carefully. "You do that a lot."

"Do what?" But I don't need him to explain. I know I spend a lot of time analyzing and overthinking things.

"Don't do that."

"Sorry."

"It's okay. But don't pretend you don't know what I'm talking about. At the risk of destroying the mood, I'm going to remind you I've had my fill of women who lie."

I close my eyes. God. I'm such an idiot. "Okay. No more deflecting."

"Attempted."

"Sorry?"

"Attempted deflecting. I see you, Oakley James. And I'm not running."

"I—" My mouth slams shut.

Am I deflecting?

In a way, yes, but with Walker it's more...a way to slow things down. I know he speaks the truth. He does see me. More clearly than anyone ever has.

He strokes a finger down my nose and draws me out of my head again. "You think deep. I like that. It means the things you do are genuine."

"I'm careful."

"I get that. It's why you're that way that has my curiosity screaming to dig and find out all your secrets, but I won't. Want to know why?"

I nod.

"Because we're going to discover everything about each other soon enough. I'll know you inside out before we're done. The reverse will also be true."

I'm still nodding because I believe him—agree with him.

"You and me are going to have an amazing life."

My throat constricts. I see the promise of his words in his eyes. Eyes that have gone completely gray, like a storm rolling in from the Gulf.

"Hey." Both his hands cradle my face. "We're in this together. One day at a time."

"I'm sorry." I sniffle. The threat of tears takes me by surprise. "I just…"

"I'm with you. It's been an emotional twenty-four hours." He grins up at me and I lean forward to press my mouth to his.

With our lips touching I say, "How has it been only twenty-four hours?"

"Yeah, feels like a lifetime to me too." His grin widens before he changes the angle of my head with his hands and slants his mouth over mine.

The kiss is a sweet exploration, a slow meld of lips, stroke of tongues, mingle of breaths.

A phone rings in the other room and I pull back. "What time is it?"

He glances at the closed curtains. "I have no idea."

Neither of us wears a watch and we left our phones in the main room of the suite after we chowed down on a midnight snack. "Those things really block shit out."

"At a guess I'd say it's at least seven."

"Oh?"

"I'm usually up at six every day. Even when I can sleep in, I'm always up by seven." He shrugs. "It feels like seven."

"Shit!" I spring up off the bed and race for the door.

"Hey! Where are you going?"

"I'm supposed to be on a call!" I yell as I throw open the bedroom door and rush across the outer room to my phone.

Snatching it up, I see I've got three missed calls, a few messages, and it's actually eight! "Double shit!"

"What? What's wrong?"

My gaze swings to the bedroom doorway where I find a very naked Walker leaning against the frame. "Ah..."

God, he's beautiful. All of him. Every last inch—

"Hey! Eyes up, Oak, what's wrong?"

"Huh?" My gaze meets his. "Oh. Right. I've missed the call. It's eight, not seven, and I'm starving." That last I add for two reasons.

One, I want to lick him up one side and down the other.

And two, my stomach is rumbling.

Our midnight snack wasn't a substitute for the dinner we both missed last night.

If we're going to do this—work together and be together—we need to stop getting distracted. Or at least not let the distractions stop us from meeting our obligations.

"My missed meeting is okay; it was only with Nat and Blake. I can call them later." I mentally run through what's on my list for today and realize the only other thing is trying to convince Walker Alcott to take the job of head coach.

It seems I'm ahead even if I'm behind.

Grinning, I head in his direction. "So, I'll reschedule my call —it was just a check-in after yesterday, and then I'll order us some breakfast. Unless you have somewhere you need to be?"

"I do. But it can wait." He pulls me into his arms. "I'd love to have breakfast with you. Spend a little more time just you and me without the world intruding."

I sigh. "That's sounds so good." My stomach rumbles again. "As you can hear, I'm starving."

"It's all that energy you expended last night. You need to refuel."

"We both do."

"Yes." His gaze is on mine, and I can tell he wants to say something else but before he does, he lets me go and taps me on the ass. "Go reschedule that call and order us some food, woman."

"Hey! You can order the food while I reschedule."

One side of his mouth kicks up in a cheeky smirk. "So I can. All right. Divide and conquer. I like it."

"What about that do you like?" I have to know if he's thinking the same thing I am.

"Us. Dividing and conquering together." His grin is wide, the sparkle in his eyes bright. "A team. We're a team."

The fact our thoughts are in line isn't a surprise. But the thrill I get when he calls us a team is. "I like that too."

"Go. Reschedule that call. I'll order breakfast, then if you don't mind, I'll plug my phone into your charger. It died last night."

"It's over there." I indicate the desk in the far corner. "I'll grab us both a robe after I message Nat and Blake."

He frowns. His gaze rolling down from my face to my feet and I can't stop the shiver that follows. "Do you have to cover up? I like this view."

It isn't until he says that that I remember the windows in this room. Spinning around, I breathe a sigh of relief to see the curtains are closed.

"Do you think I would have let you stand here naked this long if there was the remote possibility someone other than me could see you?"

My gaze moves back to Walker. The look on his face is pure possession. That dark expression, the proprietary glint of it in his eyes has a full body shudder working its way through me.

"The first thing I did when I reached that doorway was check the windows."

"Oh. I didn't even think."

"Yeah, I got that, and I couldn't think of anything else."

"Me naked or the possibility of the curtains being open?"

"Both. I know most hotels have one-way glass but I wasn't taking any chances with you."

A warmth I've only ever associated with my grandfather fills me.

Walker is taking care of me.

Sure, he took care of me in bed—and out—but that's not what this is.

This is outside of sex.

I know my friends take care of me, but the warmth I get from them isn't the same and to receive it from Walker hours after meeting him has me realizing this thing between us is far more important than anything else.

I'd pull the offer of head coach off the table if it was a choice between it or our connection.

"You're doing it again."

His words have me focusing externally—on him. "Yes. Thank you."

"For what? Worrying about you being naked in front of New York City?"

I laugh. "It's hardly the whole city but yes. For worrying about me."

He cocks his head and studies me for long seconds before he straightens and moves back to me. Cradling my face, something he seems to do a lot, he gazes into my eyes and says something no one has ever said to me before.

"I will always worry about you even when you don't need me to."

Blinking several times to alleviate the sting of tears, I can only nod.

He must see I'm struggling because he drops a kiss on my lips then changes the subject. "Is there anything you don't eat?"

"Um." I try to shift my thoughts toward food but it's hard. I'm not used to being this vulnerable—this open—with someone.

Not even my three best friends get this level of vulnerability.

And I'm giving it to Walker within hours of meeting him.

"Oak?"

"No. I don't have any allergies or dislikes."

"Okay. Go reschedule, grab us some robes, and I'll get breakfast sorted."

He's giving me a reprieve, I know he is. And as much as it pains me to admit, because I'm an independent, confident woman, I'm taking the break.

I know I'll have to think about us—what we're doing—soon enough. But for now, I want to enjoy breakfast with a man who intrigues me, gets me, in a way no other has.

Except before I do that, I need to call Nat and Blake. Or message.

If I message, I won't get stuck, and they won't see my face because I'm sure it's written all over my skin that I had the best sex of my life last night.

Pulling up our group chat, the one Cami insists she doesn't need to be a part of, I tap out a quick update.

> Sorry. Missed our call. Grabbing some breakfast before I give you all the rundown of yesterday.

After sending the message I switch my phone to silent mode. Then thinking better of it, I send a second text.

> Phone just about dead. Turning off while it charges.

It's a small lie. My battery is at sixty percent. More than enough for now but I don't want my time with Walker to end just yet and I know it will as soon as I speak to the girls.

Besides, I gave them the bare bones of the contract signing and my talk with Walker yesterday afternoon.

In that update I did mention I would be having dinner with him to discuss our offer further so they may get an inkling of why I missed this morning's call.

If not, I won't hide this thing between me and Walker from them. They need to know as much as for the sake of the franchise as for our lifelong friendship.

Well, Nat joined our group during college but for the last decade it's been the four of us against the world.

Or should I say, taking on the world.

Because that's what we've done.

And now we're taking on the male dominated world of professional sport.

I have no doubt we can do it. We're capable of anything.

We took a tiny start up, designing and sewing in the back corner of our apartment living room to the multi-billion-dollar, multi-manufacturing facilities company it is today when everyone said we'd never succeed.

And we did it on our own. We may have used some of our trust funds—and between us there are many—but Rogue paid that back within the first two years.

It helped that one of us was able to wear the brand at international sporting events all over the world. Nothing beats free advertising on an Olympic level.

Blake wore nothing but Rogue brand clothing; even when the teams she was on had other sponsors, it was in her contracts that Rogue was her sponsor and she wasn't to wear anything else.

Hell, we'd even matched colors, and styles to a degree, to whatever the teams were expected to wear.

It had cost us, but we felt the price was worth it when our name was plastered on TVs around the world.

"Hey, you done?"

I turn to see Walker leaning against the door frame again.

It's a position that does it for me for some reason. So much so, I power off my phone and drop it on the floor.

That gets me an eyebrow lift but not a comment.

Then because he has to know what I'm thinking, and if not, I'm going to give him a big hint, I sway my hips as I walk over to the bed.

"How long will breakfast be?" I ask while bending over and pressing on the bed as if testing its firmness.

"About thirty."

I face him once more. "Oh, I wonder how much more of an appetite we can work up in that time."

"Couldn't find the robes?" he asks as he slowly prowls toward me.

And it is a prowl. His limbs taut, each step measured as he draws closer, his eyes locked on his prize.

"I see something else I'd rather be wrapped in."

The smile he gives is nothing short of devious. "It's me who'll be wrapped in you."

He moves quick. Crowds me, urges me to turn back to the bed and pushes me over, and before I can catch my breath his fingers are between my legs, probing deep.

"So fucking wet."

Then his fingers are gone and in their place is the hard length of him driving into me in one long smooth stroke.

WALKER

I watch Oakley put her fork down and place a hand over her bare stomach.

I'd convinced her once our breakfast had been delivered to go without the robe.

Grinning, I sip my coffee and take in the woman across from me.

She seems to match me every step of the way. When she'd done her little temptress thing in the bedroom earlier, I'd been helpless to stop myself from taking what she offered.

And I damn well took.

Hard and fast and then again.

How either of us managed twice in thirty minutes after the number of times we'd had sex last night is anyone's guess.

Not that I'm complaining.

Nope. You won't hear a word of complaint from these lips.

"Stop staring."

"No."

She throws her head back laughing and I grin. I'm not one hundred percent sure but I'd lay money on this being an Oakley not many see.

And I'm not talking about her being naked. Her physical nakedness isn't what I'm referring to.

Last night, this morning, she's given me the privilege of seeing her unguarded. Emotionally open in a way I've never seen.

I'm honored.

Humbled.

And so damn enamored that I can't think of anything but her and fucking her again.

Both of which will happen over and over for the rest of my life if I have anything to do with it.

As I said last night, I'll give up the head coach job if it means keeping her.

"I meant what I said."

She picks up her coffee and arches an eyebrow at me. "You've said so much since we met."

I have. "I'll pass on the job if it means I can't have you."

"That won't be a choice you have to make."

"Why?"

"Because I want you to have both, and what I want, I get."

"So confident."

"I am. You know that." She takes a sip then lowers her cup to the table. "What are your plans for today?"

The change of subject doesn't bother me. I know she thinks the other topic is dealt with, and it is for us; it just remains to be seen how it goes down with the public.

With the league.

Sighing, I lower my mug and lean forward. "I know I can't say anything about the Rogues yet, so I won't, but I will be telling my sister and my best friend about my retirement and that I'll be leaving New York."

"Gannon Byrd, right?"

"Was that in your PI's report?"

"Yes. Among other things."

"Do I want to know the other things?"

She shrugs and rolls her hand to get me to answer her original question. "What else do you need to do?"

"I'll be attempting to contact Kristina to give her an ultimatum."

"Fuck off or I'll ruin you?"

I laugh. "Pretty much."

"What about the owner of the Knights?"

It's my turn to shrug. "Don't know if I'll do anything about that unless Kristina pushes my hand."

She nods. "Okay."

"Do you want to come to my place for dinner?" I don't know who's more shocked by the invite, her or me.

"Tonight?"

"Yes." The more I think about it, the more I want to see her in my space. Not that this suite isn't great but it's not personal. There's nothing of either of us here.

"Sure. What time?"

I can see she's wary but in what I'm coming to understand is typical Oakley James style, she's marching toward whatever challenge is tossed in front of her.

"How about I let you know where I am later? I've got to head to my agent's office and probably my lawyer's at some point too."

"Do you have a grill?"

"At my place?"

"No, in your pocket." She rolls her eyes at me with a laugh. "Yes, at your place. I can pick up the makings for a steak dinner if you've got somewhere to cook the steak."

I grin. Having her in my space, doing something so domestic, so couple-y, gives me a burst of joy so consuming I know I must look like an idiot.

"You like the idea of cooking dinner with me?"

"You didn't say which of us would be cooking and either one or together is perfect. Whatever you want to do."

"You can cook without assistance?"

"I had to when I moved out of home. If I wanted to maintain my body in peak form, I had to fuel it with the right meals."

She nods. "Okay, we'll cook—together—at your place tonight. Text me the address and time later and I'll pick up what we need on the way."

"All right, it's a date."

"Is that what it is?" she asks with a grin.

"It's dinner with my woman. Yes, it's a date."

"Don't dates usually require eating out?"

"We could do that but if the press release goes out this afternoon, going out will be a nightmare. Plus, I'm not sure if you want us to be seen together in public yet."

"Thanks for that consideration. I'll need to run it by Nat, Blake, and Cami before I can decide the best way to deal with the private part of our relationship. The professional connection definitely can't be revealed yet."

"Of course not. You have to announce the franchise first."

"That's slated for two weeks from today."

"Oh. So, the buzz about my retirement should have dulled by then."

"Maybe."

I could see her thinking but don't get to question her because my phone rings for what feels like the hundredth time since we sat down to breakfast.

"You should probably answer that."

I don't want to but I know she's right. Drake has been calling all morning and I didn't even bother sending him a message to let him know I'd get back to him after I ate.

Pushing back my chair, I head for the ringing device and sure enough, Drake's name is on the screen.

"Finally," Drake all but yells in my ear. "Where the hell have you been?"

"Sleeping." I glance at Oakley, a smile tugging at my mouth. "What's going on?"

"I got a call from Cantrell a couple hours ago."

"Okay."

"He wanted to let me know the team's lawyers were working on your paperwork, but we didn't need to wait for it to make your retirement announcement."

"Okay."

"Yesterday I was a little taken aback by the fact he didn't want the Knights organization to be involved in crafting your retirement announcement but I was willing to let him do things the way he saw fit—it's his team after all. Except..."

"Except what?"

"I had an itch. Today it got worse. You know, the one I get on the back of my neck? The one that's never steered me wrong."

"Yeah, I know what you're talking about." And I did—years ago, when I'd first been offered a contract, Drake had been there.

Young, and no really big clients to his name, I'd trusted his instincts because we'd been friends from my first day in college. A few years older than me, Drake had been leaning toward representing professional athletes instead of pushing to be one himself. He'd had talent, but in his words, not enough to get far, not as far as he could help someone else get.

"What did you do?" I ask even though I know he'll tell me anyway.

"I had our lawyers pull your latest contract. Got them to comb over that fucker from first word to last."

"And?" There is an edge to my voice because I know he's found something with the number of calls and texts I've missed from him this morning.

"And that motherfucker is trying to get you to breach your contract."

"How?"

"There's a clause about termination; I won't bore you with the legalese but basically, you can't make an announcement of any kind, including the current status of your injury—only the team can. If you do, you're in breach, and he can sue the ass off you."

"Isn't there some sort of clause about me suing the team over my career-ending injury?"

"No. There's a clause that gives you a mass payout if you're unable to continue playing due to injury caused while performing your job but that too would be void if we put out a press release about your retirement."

"So what does this mean?" I hate that Cantrell has us over a barrel.

"Well, until we get the paperwork from the Knights org, our hands are tied, and we have to zip our lips."

"And how long with that take?" I glance at Oakley again. I want to move forward with the Rogues, but I can't do that until I end things with the Knights.

Drake sighs. "I've got a feeling that fucker is going to drag this out."

"So what? I'm stuck in limbo, can't go back, can't go forward, until he sees fit to pull his head out of his ass?"

"Basically, yeah."

"Fucker!"

"Hey." Oakley puts her hand on my arm. "What's going on?" she whispers.

"Who's that?" Drake asks.

"Hang on a sec," I tell him.

I place my hand over the bottom of my phone, bring it down to my chest, and keep my voice low.

"Cantrell is being a dick. I can't sign anything with you until the announcement goes out and I can't announce without all the Is dotted and Ts crossed."

"Use the pictures."

"Huh?" For a second I have no idea what she's talking about, and then it hits me.

The pictures of Cantrell and Kristina.

Bringing the phone back to my ear I speak to Drake.

"Get everything you need to terminate my contract with the Knights and the statement about my retirement ready. And find

Cantrell. I want to know where he is, who he's with, within the hour. I'll get whatever we need from the team by this afternoon."

"How? You can't punch him if that's what you're planning. Although, to be honest, I wouldn't mind you doing that, wouldn't mind slugging the guy myself."

"I'm not going to hit him." I scrub a hand down my face. "I've got an incentive for him to get things moving and moving fast."

"What kind of incentive?"

I look at Oakley. The woman has saved me twice in the last twenty-four hours. First with a job offer and now with the solution to this bullshit with Cantrell.

"Just something I know he won't want anyone else knowing."

"You've got dirt on Cantrell? Jesus fuck, man, what the hell could you have on him? I know he's a sleaze and all, but I've never even heard a rumor about the guy that could be used against him."

"No rumors and I'm not giving you details. Just get everything ready and find out where the fuck that prick is. I'm catching up with Shelby for lunch and then I'm going after Cantrell."

I hang up on Drake before he can dig any further. I don't want him implicated in any way with this.

Same with Oakley.

"Those pictures can't be linked back to you, can they?"

"No. But even if they can, I'm not worried about it."

"How can you not be worried?" I grab her shoulders. "This could fuck up the franchise."

"No. That's a done deal and the Rogues organization employed the PI to investigate a number of individuals we're looking at employing. From the Zamboni driver to the window washers, everyone will or has been looked into."

"Wow. Okay, I see how that could be okay. You were looking at me, and Kristina is linked to—"

"Not anymore."

"Not for a while but it does seem logical as to how you might have come about having these in your possession."

"Now they're in yours and you need to use them to your advantage."

"First I need to tell Shelby I'm leaving New York."

"Will that be a problem? I know she recently finished college. Will she come with you?"

I shake my head. "No. She already has a job. Although this move will give me the upper hand in getting her to move into my apartment. Without me living there, she's more likely to say yes."

"She's an independent girl."

"Yes. Our parents' deaths have a lot to do with that, I think."

"I don't know, I think maybe you're both cut from the same cloth and go after what you want on your own merit."

"The fact she won't use my name to get in the door at the Knights' head office is in the report?"

I'd tried to convince Shelby to work for the Knights. Mischa had offered when she found out Shel was studying PR, but my sister doesn't want a job because of who her brother is, she wants one because she's good.

"No. But from what I've read about both of you, and what I've learned in the last twenty-four hours about you, makes me believe you would want to help her."

"I did. Do. Do the Rogues need anyone in the PR department?"

Oakley laughs and I want to kiss the sound from her lips.

So I do.

And as much as I try to keep it tame, the way we combust every time we come together can't be controlled.

Within seconds I'm taking us both to the floor. We're already naked and this area of the suite has plush carpet but I roll us so I'm on the bottom.

Against her lips I say, "You're on top. Do your worst."

"You mean my best?" She nips my lip. Slides her tongue over the small sting.

"I think we've proven the only thing we are together is the best," I murmur as I trail my mouth along her jawline.

She stops, pulls back, and looks at me. "Together we're the best."

I eye her, wondering what it is she's working on in her head. I don't have to wait long for her brain to tie all the strings and deliver her conclusion.

"We're going public."

"What?" I sit up, Oakley straddling my lap.

"Hear me out. We met at the photo shoot. Yesterday. We got together for dinner last night. Will again tonight."

"Okay." I'm not sure where she's going with this line of thinking, but I give her the chance to sort through it more.

Honestly, I don't care how this all goes down as long as it's the least amount of damage to her and the Rogues.

To distract us both, I run my tongue over one peaked nipple. The shiver that shakes her makes me smile and I open my mouth around the taut bud and suck hard.

Her back arches, her flesh pressing deeper into my mouth, and I greedily suck it down.

It takes little effort from either of us for me to get inside her. A little wiggling, a shift up then down and I'm balls deep in snug wet heat.

"Fuck. So tight. So wet," I growl over her skin as I move to her other breast.

"I'm tight because you're big."

I can't help the laugh that breaks free. "Just what every guy wants to hear."

"I speak only the truth."

"Why are you speaking at all, woman? Ride me." I give her ass a slap and the next thing I know I'm flat on my back, her palms pressing into my chest, and she's riding me like the prize-winning jockey at the Kentucky Derby.

I fuck up into her as best I can but she's driving this ride. And what a ride it is.

It has sweat dripping from both of us. And I'm sure my ass is going to have rug burn but I don't care. I'll take the pain as a badge of honor that this woman knows she's safe with me to let herself go.

Safe to take what she wants and needs and—

"Fuck!"

Her pussy locks down on my cock in a painful grip that sucks my orgasm right out of me.

I'm gasping for air, my fingers digging into the flesh of her ass while I hold on. To her. To my sanity.

This woman.

I've never experienced anything like this. I'm burning from the inside out and the outside in, and I never want it to stop.

OAKLEY

The second the suite door closes behind Walker, I head for the bedroom.

I need to shower and get dressed.

It's not like I'm worried about Nat or Blake seeing me in a robe, but I want to show them whatever is happening between me and Walker will not affect the businesswoman.

I don't think they'll be a hard sell when it comes to mine and Walker's personal relationship but I'd still prefer to show them there isn't going to be a problem before they can question it.

My phone beeps. Glancing at the screen I see a message from Walker.

Haven't been gone a minute and I miss you.

I can't stop a smile from stretching my lips. I'm opening the message to reply when another one comes in.

It's too much, right?

Followed by another.

It's weird to feel this attached so quickly.

I hurry my reply because I don't want him to feel like he's the only one in this.

Same. No. Yes, but I'm with you.

I think about our conversation for a second.

Everything we've said is true. I do miss him, it doesn't feel like it's too much, and yes, I'm one hundred percent in this with him.

It's scary how connected I feel, how comfortable I feel with that connection while still being a little scared of it.

Even with how new this thing is with Walker, I'm more invested than I ever have been with a man.

Toss in the fact I'm going to be working closely with him to prove the world wrong about a typically male-dominated profession and I—*we*—have every right to be scared.

I'm not backing away though. I can't. Not after last night.

Or this morning.

If he hadn't come here, hadn't been as unable to deny our chemistry as I was, then maybe.

Maybe I could back away and let the Rogues take center stage.

Except my gut tells me we'll work better if we pursue both.

And yes, I mean we. We both have to be in this for it to work. I'm confident Walker is. I know I am.

Everything I learned about him from the PI report only solidifies my opinion of him. He's dedicated, doesn't buckle under pressure or responsibility, and is not afraid to handle a change of direction.

He might have had some concerns about his career—or the change to it—but the way he stood up and took care of his sister after their parents died tells me he's more than capable of making this shift from player to coach.

> Heading to see Shelby. Gannon too. I won't
> mention the details, but I'll tell them about a
> job taking me out of New York.

I smile at Walker's latest text. He's made it clear, numerous times, he'll be telling his sister, and he promised me Gannon could be trusted.

I wanted to tell him I knew Gannon was trustworthy but then I'd have to reveal he's one of the players on our list. As much as I want Walker diving into his role, he still has to sign a contract.

And I want him to concentrate on extricating himself from the Knights.

Jerry Cantrell is going to be a problem. I have a connection I can use, one that might nudge Cantrell in the right direction, but I'm not ready to use it.

Walker has the pictures. He can use those to push Cantrell. If that doesn't work, then I'll step in, and as Walker's girlfriend and future boss I will do that, even if it is blurring the lines between personal and professional.

Which reminds me I need to move it so I can get the call with Nat and Blake happening. We'll need to brainstorm my plan, check dates, see what we can line up and what won't.

As I rush through my shower, my mind rolls. I'm running through my travel for the last few months, seeing if I can remember how many times I've been in New York.

I'm sure there are several that would match Walker's location. I need Trevor to send me the last twelve months of my movements so I can compare it to Walker's.

I need to make that request to my assistant over the phone. I don't want a trail someone could stumble upon to derail my plan.

Of course, I have to let the girls know what I'm planning. Cami should be involved too but I know she'll object and tell me to do whatever.

As much as I love that woman, her lack of interest in the day to day running of either of our businesses is frustrating. She's happy to just hand over money and let us do whatever with it.

In her words, 'why should I get involved when you three know what you're doing and do it so well', and she's not wrong.

Nat, Blake and I have been the driving force behind Rogue sportswear and now we're spearheading the Rogues hockey franchise.

Out of the shower, I debate which suit to wear. I want something that screams I'm in control even if I can be—have been—out of control in front of my best friends before.

The three women who make up the rest of KAW have always had my back. As I've had theirs. We've stood side by side and faced all the challenges that have come our way.

And to think, it all started on a wine-fueled night in a tiny apartment where the four of us were lamenting the stigma we faced for being 'trust-fund' babies.

Blake had been the only one without that hanging around her neck, but she'd had different loads to bear. Being the only daughter of a hockey god playing a sport typically male dominated comes with its own dramas and difficulties.

I laugh when I remember Cami thrusting her glass in the air, wine sloshing over the sides and screaming at the top of her lungs, "Fuck them all! We're kick-ass women and we'll prove it!"

We've never revealed where we got the name for our company. And we don't intend to. Well, maybe we will when we're in our seventies and we've finished taking on the world.

Reaching for my blood red skirt, I pair it with a gold silk blouse and a blue blazer. Staring at my reflection, I ponder the color combo.

And the more I look, the more I think I've found our team colors. Snapping a pic with my phone, I send it to all three of my best friends with a question.

Rogues team colors?

Nat is the first to reply.

Yes!

Then Blake.

Maybe tone the red down a little

I wait for Cami's opinion. And laugh at myself when I realize she won't bother replying because it's a business decision and she's determined to stay out of those.

You look good. Glowing. Did you get laid?

I stand, mouth agape, rereading Cami's text. Scrolling back up the thread I stare at the picture.

Holy shit.

She's right. I'm kind of glowing.

I could blame it on the lighting or the outfit or even the pleasure of signing the contract with the NHL but I know that's all a lie.

It's Walker.

It's all the great, incredible, fantastic sex.

It's the thought of seeing him tonight.

I can't keep this feeling in. There's no way I'll be able to pretend there's nothing between me and Walker.

And that thought just confirms what I've spent the morning rolling around my head.

We need to go public with our relationship before we announce the Rogues franchise or the coaching staff.

Luckily we have a few weeks before the team announcement and a few more weeks after that before we'll announce the coaches.

> Call in five. Cami, you aren't getting out of this one. I NEED you on it!

With that directive sent, I head out to where my laptop is set up and get it powered on. I need to make a quick call to Trevor first.

He answers on the first ring. "Yo, boss lady."

"I need you to send me my complete calendar going back twelve months. Personal and business."

"Okay." I can hear him tapping away. "Can I ask why?"

"Yes, but you can't write it down anywhere or tell anyone else."

"My lips are always sealed when it comes to you."

"See if you can get me Walker Alcott's whereabouts for the same time."

"On it. Although that might be a bit trickier to come by without leaving a trace or a rumor."

"Pull what you can from the PI report, and I'll get the rest."

"Anything else? Do you need me to confirm your flight out tomorrow?"

"Shit. No. Cancel that—wait. No. Leave it as is for now. I'll let you know later today but I might stay longer than planned. Actually, I might need you to come up here..."

"I'll pack a bag just in case."

"Thanks, Trevor. You're invaluable."

"You pay me to be invaluable."

"I do, but it's not so you are, it's because you are."

"Oh, flattery will get you everywhere."

I laugh. "I don't need flattery for that."

"No. You don't. But enough of this sentimental crap, back to work. You've got a world to take over."

"I do. I'll check in later cand let you know what to do about the flight."

"Did you know you've been in New York every month in the

last year?" he asks. "Hmm... I didn't realize it had been that many times."

"I needed to be in their faces to pull this off."

"You didn't, but I get why you think you did."

I glance at my laptop and see Nat has sent the link for the call. "Gotta go, got a KAW powwow happening in one."

"Later." Trevor hangs up before I can and I'm switching my phone to silent and clicking through to the call at the same time. "Hel—"

"I fucked Walker," the words fly out of my mouth before I think them. Dammit. I wanted to ease them into this.

"Okay..." Nat eyes me with her usual probing gaze. "Does this mean we're back to square one on the head coach front?"

"No. He said yes to that, but he's got some things to sort out before he can sign."

"And you and he hooked up?" asks Blake.

"Yes. No." I rub my forehead. "It's more than that."

"Why am I here for this?" Cami asks as she pops up on my screen.

"You missed the best bit!" Blake laughs.

"What bit? I know she signed the contract with the league, I know we're going ahead with the Rogues."

"Yes, but your comment about her glow was spot on," Nat adds.

"Oh? You got laid?" Cami gives me a slow clap. "About damn time."

"Hey! It hasn't been that long. And I've been busy with better things."

"Anything that puts a glow like that on your face is the best thing." Cami sighs. "I wish I could find me some glow."

"You'd need a guy for that." Blake frowns, "I could do with a guy for that too."

"I have a guy and let me tell you, there's none of that there."

I have to bite my tongue at the mention of Nat's husband.

He's a leech. One that she continues to put up with. I'm almost at my patience's end when it comes to that man.

We all are.

A number of times over the years, he's tried to derail Nat's success. I'm sure he's going to prove a pain in the ass once he finds out about the Rogues. I still don't know how she's managed to keep it from him.

"Okay. So here's the plan. I'm getting the info together but we're going to go public with our relationship. We'll make it look as though we've been seeing each other for a few months, maybe a year, although that might be hard with his ex and his injury so it might be best to place our timeline to just after he took the hit."

"No one would believe you weren't by his side when he ended up in the hospital," Blake adds. "I'd definitely go with getting together after that."

"All right. I'm having dinner with him tonight and we'll go over both our movements for the last twelve months to see when we were in the same place."

"You've been up there a lot," Cami says. "You could easily have been spending time with him."

"Exactly. Now the other problem is that Cantrell is up to something. I'm not sure of the exact details but I've given Walker those pictures to remove Kristina from his life, and they'll work just as well for Cantrell."

"Is it a contract clause?" Nat asks. I can see she's madly tapping away on her keyboard.

"I think so. He was set to announce his retirement today but from what he said that's on hold until he meets with Cantrell," I explain. "He also needs to tell his sister and he'll be telling Gannon Byrd at the same time."

"You didn't tell him we're looking at Byrd, did you?" Blake asks.

"No. I also didn't tell him what the PI discovered about his best friend and little sister."

"Good call. He'll find out when they want him to find out." Cami nods. "We shouldn't play god with that info."

I arch an eyebrow at her. "Since when do you know what's in the PI reports?"

"I might not want in on the day-to-day decisions but I know what's going on. Well, as much as I'm able to when I have a job outside of the company."

"Compan*ies*. Plural. We have two now." I grin.

All three of them match my smile.

"We certainly do," Nat murmurs. "Oh. I think I found what the problem with Cantrell is. Was Walker planning to make his retirement announcement himself?"

I'm nodding before she finishes speaking. "Yes."

"Whose idea was that?"

"Not sure but I think Cantrell told him yesterday to go ahead and announce."

"Oh, that fucker. Can we take him out with the info we have?" Nat asks.

"Not yet." I'm shaking my head now. "Let's see if Walker can get himself clear first."

"Good idea. We don't want our hands in too much muck before we even get blades on the ice," Blake adds. "I can maybe get Dad or one of my brothers to do the dirty work there."

"Let's see how things go. Oh, and I'll probably be here a few more days. I'm not sure how long yet. It will depend on when Walker can get himself clear of the Knights and I get his sig on our contract."

"Take all the time you need. We've got everything handled down here and if we need an extra body, I'll drag Cami's ass in," Nat says.

"Hey!"

"You'll do it." Nat glares at the screen.

"Of course I will." Cami rolls her eyes. "I'd rather not but I will if I have to."

"Good. All right. I think that's it for now. I'll keep you updated."

"By phone. No messages or emails." Nat reminds us all that what we're talking about needs to remain between us.

"Let me know when Walker is ready to talk players. I've got something in mind that we'll need to get on right away," Blake says.

"Will do." I look at the time. "I need to make a few calls to our designers. I'll be emailing you all some of the photos from yesterday's shoot. I think we might have a small issue with the full suit."

"Oh?" Nat pulls her attention away from whatever she was doing back to me.

"Yeah, it was like he was naked once he started to sweat in it. Take a look at the pictures and let me know what you think."

"Okay. Anything else?" Nat asks, her eyes bouncing between what must be the three of us on her screen.

"Nope. I've got nothing."

"I've just got what I'll be emailing about the new line."

"Do you even need me to answer?" Cami asks with a grin.

Nat rolls her eyes and disconnects.

Laughing, Cami says, "Well, goodbye to you too, Nat."

"Talk later." Blake logs out, leaving just me and Cami.

"Are you good?" she asks.

"Yeah. More than good. The connection is unreal."

"Explains the glow."

"Probably. Anyway, I gotta go. I'm behind."

"That's what happens when you have a hot guy in your bed that makes you glow." Cami grins before cutting our connection.

I can't argue with her words, although I will nag her about her lack of goodbye.

Smiling, I click out of our call and open up my email. The first thing I see is that Trevor has already sent me my calendar for the last year.

I'm itching to get in and work out the details of my and Walker's relationship but I've got other work that needs to be done first.

Besides, I'd rather make those rendezvous with the man himself.

WALKER

I hang up on the call when Shelby's phone kicks over to voicemail. Again.

This is the third time I've tried and I'm starting to worry. I shouldn't, I know she's an adult and has a life and can't always pick up when her brother calls.

Changing my plans, I lean forward and direct the driver to Gannon's place. I'll keep trying my sister, but I'll get my best friend first.

It might be better to tell them together anyway. Me leaving New York affects them equally. Gannon might not be blood related but he's a brother to me. Has been since the first day we met in college.

And he was a rock when our parents died and Shel had to come live with me.

Shooting a text to my sister telling her to meet me at Gannon's or call me asap, I lean back and think about what I can tell them.

I know neither of them would blab to the media, but I signed an NDA and I'm not about to break that. Even if Oakley would be okay with me revealing where I'm going.

No. The only thing I'll tell them is I'm leaving New York

for a job offer. I'll lead with my retirement of course—it's the main reason I need to speak to them both before we make it public.

I glance at my phone hoping Drake has gotten back to me about Cantrell's whereabouts.

If I haven't heard from Drake by the time I leave Gannon's, I'll call Rafe and find out where I might locate the Knights owner.

It's another twenty minutes of weaving in and out of New York traffic before the cab pulls up in front of Gannon's building. I don't even look as I toss money at the driver and get out.

I'm halfway to the front door when I hear my name. Turning I see my sister waving her arm to get my attention. Then I notice the man next to her, the tension in my shoulders seems to melt down my spine as a sigh of relief leaves my lungs.

I wait where I am. No point heading to them. They just have to come here anyway.

"Hey, man," Gannon says.

I hold up my fist for a bump as I say, "Hey." Then I slip an arm around Shel and give her a squeeze. "Let's go up. I've got something I need to tell you both."

"Sounds serious," Shelby says as I usher her into the foyer of Gannon's building. "Everything okay?"

"Yeah. All good." And I mean it. It might be bad that my playing career is over but I'm good. Excited about the future. Which I probably shouldn't be when I think about it. "Just some news that will hit the media in the next forty-eight hours I want you guys to hear from me first."

Shel glances at Gannon and they share a look I can't quite interpret but I'm sure it's worry. We need to get upstairs so I can put their concerns aside.

We're quiet on the elevator ride up and it's not until we get inside Gannon's place that anyone says a word. And they're not the words I figured would be said because the first thing I see when I enter the apartment is Shelby's suitcases in the living room.

"Is this your stuff?" I ask with a little confusion. She's supposed to be in her apartment for a few more weeks.

"Yes! Isn't it cool!" My sister's voice is a little loud but I put it down to the excitement I can see in her eyes. "Gannon offered to rent me a spare room so I don't have to worry about finding a place of my own and this way I get the best of both worlds—I get to live on my own but still have a roommate."

Shel is grinning at me with such joy and with me moving out of New York I have to agree with her, this is the best outcome—aside from her moving into my place—I could hope for.

"Really? That's great. You have no idea how worried I've been."

I see them share another look but before I can explain, Shelby is talking.

"Why were you worried? You knew I'd be moving out of the shared apartment; we've talked about it a lot."

Taking a step toward her I say, "Oh, no, not about you moving. About..." I glance at Gannon before turning back to Shel. "I'm. I. Shit."

"What?" Shelby grabs both my hands. "What's wrong? Tell me. Whatever it is, I'm sure it'll be all right."

"So much is changing," I manage through my constricting throat.

"That's life, it's always changing but what won't change is our support of you. Wherever it is, we will both be beside you," Gannon says as he moves closer.

And before I can think better of it, I blurt, "I'm retiring. And moving."

"I. Sorry? What? Moving?" Shelby mumbles.

I laugh. "Out of that it's the moving that got you?"

"Well, yeah, it doesn't seem like a big deal. Gannon moved here a couple of years ago," Shel adds with a shrug.

"I'm retiring from playing," I repeat to be sure she heard that part. "But I'm not retiring from professional hockey."

"Are you joining the team's couching staff?"

I'm not surprised Gannon voices the question. He understands the workings of a team and a few players move from playing to coaching or elsewhere in a hockey org.

"No." Then I add something I'm sure he'll pick up on. "Not for your team."

Sure enough, his eyebrows rise, and he asks, "My team?"

"Yes, as of yesterday I'm no longer contracted to New York. And I can't say for who or where my new job will be but it's not here."

"Oh, you're leaving New York?" Shelby's eyes fill with tears and her mouth scrunches in the way it usually does when she's about to cry. "We won't live near each other anymore?"

"No. So I'm really, *really* glad you're sharing with Gannon. I won't have to worry about you being on your own when I'm gone."

"Even if she hadn't moved in here, she wouldn't be on her own," Gannon says, his voice a little angry.

"Yes, yes, I know but this is better." I smile to show I'm more than happy with him being there for my sister. "Now I need to go. I've got stuff to organize and while I can't tell you where I'm going yet, I will as soon as I get the green light on that. My retirement announcement goes out to the media today so it'll either hit tomorrow or the next day."

"More like tonight. Especially if Drake is sending it wide and not just to specific media outlets," Gannon says.

"It's going wide. We offered the organization the right to announce but they refused. Another thing I need to do, sort out the clusterfuck that is the termination of my contract." I shake my head. "Anyway, I'll get out of your hair so you two can get Shelby settled. I'll call you both later."

I'm out the door without even a goodbye, never mind a hug for my sister or a fist bump for my best friend. But I'm on a mission. And my phone has been going off in my pocket so I can only assume—hope—Drake has discovered where Cantrell is.

I step into the elevator before I pull my phone from my pocket. I've got several missed calls and a couple of texts.

It's the text I zero in on because they're all from Drake and yes, the man has come through and found out where I can find Jerry Cantrell.

Unfortunately it's in a place I don't really want to go. For long minutes I debate what to do. I don't want to see Kristina. But then if I can confront them together, I can kill two birds with one stone and get back to Oakley quicker.

I'm on the sidewalk waving down a cab when another text comes in from Drake.

> They're headed out. And a little birdie tells me they're on their way to Maguire's.

I stare at the message long enough the cabbie toots his horn and yells, "You getting in?"

Shaken out of my shock, I yank open the rear door and jump in. "Yeah. Sorry. You know where Maguire's is?"

"Who doesn't? You going there?"

"Yeah, seems that way."

I can't believe Cantrell is heading to one of the hottest restaurants in New York with Kristina. Does he not understand what being seen with her in an intimate setting like Maguire's will say about them?

Unlocking my phone, I send a quick thank you text to Drake then open my browser and search Cantrell's name. Nothing comes up that makes me think him being seen in public with Kristina is acceptable.

My next search is Laken Cantrell. Nothing pops up. Nothing when I search the New York Knights either. Or Kristina.

I have no idea what I'm walking into, but I do know what I'll be walking out with.

Kristina will be out of my life and Cantrell will get the team lawyers or GM or whoever to release me from my contract so I can make my retirement announcement.

Hell, at this point the Knights org can make the announcement. I don't care. I just want it done. Today.

When the cab pulls up out front of the restaurant, I can see my quarry sitting right in the window.

I take my time paying the driver. The whole time I'm studying the two of them together.

If you didn't know who they were, you'd think they were a couple. Neither of them is taking notice of anyone else but as I get out of the cab I see two others join them.

Laken Cantrell and New York's GM, Rafferty 'Rafe' King.

Stepping to the side, I take my time watching. It's a weird combination of table occupants.

Laken and Cantrell I get—they're husband and wife—and maybe I can understand Rafe being there too, but Kristina?

How the fuck does she play into this late lunch date?

Deciding I've waited long enough, I move toward the front door. Inside the hostess barely bats an eye as I move past her and head for the table of four.

Scooping up an empty chair from the table beside theirs, I spin it around and straddle it backward. "Afternoon. This is an interesting get together."

"Alcott. What the—" Cantrell sucks in a breath. "What are you doing here?"

"I'll ask you the same. But I'll add 'here with my ex who has been harassing me for months'," I say with a smirk.

"I, I, I," Cantrell sputters.

"It's because I'm worried about you," Kristina says. "I asked Jerry to meet with me so we can do something to help you."

I laugh. I can't help it. This bullshit just keeps getting deeper.

Pulling in a breath I lean forward. "You and I both know

that's a lie and so does he." I hook my thumb in Cantrell's direction.

"It's no—"

"Zip it. I'm speaking and you're listening. You will not contact me ever again. You will remove any evidence that we even know each other and that includes changing your fucking mailing address back to your own. And you!" I stab a finger in Cantrell's direction. "You will get up from here and head straight to the Knights head office and get my contract terminated the way it should be. The way I deserve it to be."

"Excuse me." Mrs. Cantrell places her hand on my arm. "What's this about your contract?"

I glance at her, then at Rafe. "I had a meeting with your husband yesterday about it."

"And I wasn't informed? Were you, Rafe?"

"Yes. But not until after because I was with Bryson in the ER getting his broken arm set."

"You told me about Bryson but didn't mention anything about the meeting. Are you aware of what Walker is talking about?"

"I am. But obviously I'm missing some details. Care to elaborate, Jer?"

Cantrell visibly bristles at the shortening of his name. Or maybe it's the way Rafe says it, with loathing clearly coating it.

Sitting up straight, I watch the daggers arrow across the table. For a few seconds I wait. But when no one speaks, and let's be real, it should be Cantrell who speaks, I decide to provide the details.

But not before I remove us from the very public place we're currently in. "Rafe, Mrs. Cantrell, if you'd please come with me to finish this conversation in private."

"You're not going anywhere!" Cantrell's hand slams down on his wife's shoulder.

I'm so shocked, I can't speak.

Not so Rafe. Through clenched teeth he growls, "Get your fucking hand off her or I'll remove it."

Cantrell immediately removes his hand, he even cradles it under his opposite arm. Does he think Rafe is going to launch across the table and cut it off with his butter knife?

Mrs. Cantrell rises from her seat. "If you'll follow me, Walker. Rafe."

To my surprise we leave the other two at the table. I glance back once to see Kristina leaning toward Cantrell frantically talking and gesturing.

"I'll have my car brought around. We can talk there in privacy."

"Okay." I look at Rafe. "How's your son?"

"Plastered to the elbow and unable to play hockey for six weeks but otherwise he's fine."

"On ice accident?" I ask.

"No. Locker room, after the game. A few of them were goofing off and three ended up with broken bones." Rafe rolls his eyes heavenward. "I swear, the boy and his friends will be the death of me."

"I'm sure he won't. He's the best part of your life, Rafe, and you love his boisterous ways." Mrs. Cantrell points to a large black SUV pulling up. "This is us."

Rafe opens the door and says with a grin, "Yes, he is, and I do."

I follow them both inside and don't wait for the vehicle to pull away before I'm replaying yesterday's meeting.

"My agent and I had a meeting with Mr. Cantrell yesterday to inform the team that as a result of the injuries I sustained while playing, I'm unable to play any longer and am retiring. He assured us we could make my retirement announcement only for us to discover today that if I do, the Knights org will be able to sue me for breach of contract."

"He didn't." Rafe's jaw clenches. Then he turns to Mrs. Cantrell. "I think it's time we pull the ace in our hand."

"Yes. It appears so."

"It'll be fine. I'll be with you every step of the way."

I'm not sure what is happening here but these two seem to have a far deeper relationship than I'm aware off.

"Look, I'm not sure…" I glance at Cantrell's wife.

"You can be candid. Laken is aware of her husband's faults. *All* of them."

"Ah, well, um."

"Walker, please, be honest with us. Think of this vehicle as a vault."

"What I have doesn't necessarily need to stay locked in here."

"Okay. But before you start, let me assure you there will be no repercussions for you from the Knights. And I guarantee after you leave this car, the first thing I will do is contact our lawyers and have any paperwork required to terminate your contract done with a legal document saying the Knights give you permission to announce your retirement as you see fit."

I glance at Rafe. I've never known Mrs. Cantrell to be involved in the running of the team. Rafe as GM has always been what his title says, the manager.

Except on the rare occasion that Cantrell himself got involved. Of course, unlike yesterday, those times Rafe was there to override or guide him.

"This information does not leave this vehicle until it is made public." Rafe's stare drills into me.

I nod. "Of course."

"Jerry Cantrell doesn't actually own the Knights. Gerald Senior left the team to Laken."

"But—"

"Jerry doesn't know," Mrs. Cantrell adds. "And I'm in the process of organizing things so that I can sever any and all ties with my husband."

"Oh. Well, you might need or want what I have to aid that."

"And what is it that you have, Walker?"

"Pictures of him and Kristina Bancroft in compromising positions."

"How did you get those?" Rafe asks.

"Ah, that's something I cannot tell you, but they are authentic."

"Oh, I have no doubt they are." Mrs. Cantrell shakes her head. "He's such an idiot."

"No argument here," Rafe adds.

"So, can I get my agent to craft my retirement announcement today and send it out first thing tomorrow?"

"You can send it today, Walker. The minute you step out I'll be on the phone, but I will personally call your agent the minute the paperwork is signed." Mrs. Cantrell holds out her hand. "It's been a pleasure having you on the team, and I wish you the best in the future."

I take her hand, surprised by the strength of her shake. Rafe offers his hand next.

"You need anything else, call me or Laken personally."

"Thank you. Both. Where do you want me to send those pictures?"

"I'll be in touch about those in the next few days."

"Okay." I grab the door handle but look back to say, "And, Mrs. Cantrell, I hope you get to sever those ties fast and cleanly."

"I appreciate the thought, but you know Jerry."

The smile she gives me says it all. Her husband isn't going to go away easily and what that means for the Knights is anyone's guess.

Good thing as of tomorrow, I'll be free to join the Rogues and leave all the drama behind me.

OAKLEY

I check my phone one more time to be sure I've got the right address. The small grocery store on the corner doesn't look large enough to offer more than snacks but it's where Walker said to meet him.

Thanking the driver, I hop out of the car and glance around to see if Walker is here yet.

We said four but it's only five to, so I'm not surprised I don't see him.

Moving toward the store, I stand off to the left of the door and pull out my phone. I wrote a list of things to get for dinner but now I'm wondering if I'll have to rework it.

I didn't think I was being extravagant in my choice of meal when I decided what we'd have, and I still don't think I am except now I'm rethinking it because of the small store behind me.

"Hey."

My head snaps up to find Walker standing in front of me. How he got there, so close, without me noticing is a worry but it doesn't stop the smile spreading across my face. "Hey."

He reaches for me, and quickly has me in his arms, his mouth on mine.

The kiss is a little passionate for a public street although I can't seem to care about that when he's touching me.

I have a plan.

I know I have a plan.

I just can't remember what that is right now...

He pulls away and rests his forehead on mine. "Damn. I needed that."

"Bad day?"

"Strange day."

"You get everything sorted out?" The worry I feel is for him, not that he might be tied up and unable to join the Rogues yet.

"Yes. We could have released the announcement this afternoon, but I've asked Drake to hold off until tomorrow. I wanted to speak to you first."

"Oh?" I'm surprised he wants to talk to me about it. "Why?"

"Because I don't want it to conflict with anything you have planned. I know you were hatching something all day, and I'll slide into that plan wherever you think is best."

"Ah, right. Okay, let's get the groceries for dinner and head to your place. We can go over everything while we cook."

"*We're* cooking?" Walker entwines his fingers with mine and tugs me toward the store.

"Yes. Although I'm rethinking my choice of meal," I say as he pulls me through the doorway.

"You wanted to grill, right? They have great steaks here and their veggie choice is always fresh and varied."

He scoops up a basket as we pass the stack and leads me straight toward the back. "You shop here a lot?" I ask looking at the shelves as we pass. He's right about variety. There's plenty in this aisle.

"Yes. They're open early 'til late so it fits with my schedule." He stops us in front of a refrigerator filled with meat. "Now where... Ah, here."

I have to step back or get smacked in the face with the door when he yanks it open. He picks out a tray of two steaks, New York cut, and drops it in the basket.

"I'm thinking grilled zucchini and eggplant plus a Greek salad. Do you want baked potatoes to go with it?" he asks over his shoulder as he heads off again.

"Um, sure." Looks like I shouldn't have bothered writing a list. Walker has it all sorted.

I follow him through the store and watch as he carefully picks two zucchini then an eggplant before moving on to the potatoes.

When he heads toward the front of the store, away from the fresh veg I ask, "Don't we need stuff for the Greek salad?"

"No, I have all that at home. The dressing too. It's one of my staples. I'm not a big salad fan but I can handle a Greek one. Sometimes I bastardize it but it's still kind of the same."

"Bastardize?"

"Yeah, it's where you twist something from its original form. This time it means a change of ingredients."

"You are full of surprises."

He grins at me. "Do you like surprises?"

"It wouldn't matter if I didn't because I like you."

His grin softens, more of an affectionate smile now instead of a cocky smirk. "I like you too, Oak."

"Hello, Mr. Walker." The teenager behind the counter smiles with worshipful eyes at Walker.

"Hey, Danny. How's your mom doing?"

"Better. She should be back at work soon. Once she gets her walking cast on, she can handle the register. Grandpa won't let her even enter the shop before then."

The kid grins and the love he has for both relatives is evident in his eyes.

"Is this it or do you want to keep shopping?"

"This is it. Oh, and can I put a hold on my next delivery?"

"Sure." The kid starts to run everything through the scanner. "Oh, I forgot to tell you last time, Grandpa said to thank you for the tickets and for the word of mouth."

"Anytime. Tell Grandpa I'll come see him soon."

"He's in back now but he's arguing with a supplier so I don't want to disturb him."

"No, don't interrupt him. He's fierce as a shark when he's haggling."

"He's trying to teach me, but I don't want to work here forever."

"You still want to play pro?"

"Of course! It's all I've ever wanted."

"How are you doing on the ice?" Walker pulls out his wallet and hands over a card.

"I'm the fastest on the team." Danny's chest puffs out. "And my coach said I've got talent."

"I know you do. How about I hook you up with some guys to show you some pro tips?"

"I, you, huh?" Danny's mouth flaps as he tries to get words out and I have to hide my smile by turning away.

"I'll get you set up soon." Walker takes the bag of groceries from Danny. "And keep doing those exercises I taught you for off ice."

"Every day. Even when I'm sick, I do them."

"No need to do that. You need to take care of your body because if you go pro, it'll take a beating. Hell, it'll take one before that, so if you're sick, modify your workout."

"Okay. I will. Thanks, Mr. Walker."

"You're welcome, Danny. Take care of your mom."

Danny groans. "You sound like Grandpa."

"He knows what he's talking about."

"Yeah, but you all don't need to remind me to take care of her. She's the only one I got."

Sadness moves across Danny's face and Walker reaches over with his free hand and claps him on the shoulder. "Your dad would be proud of you. He *was* proud of you."

"I know." Danny gulped. "I wish..."

"We all do." Walker gives Danny's shoulder a squeeze then

glances at me. "Gotta get going. Need to get my girl home and feed her dinner."

Danny grins in a way I'm sure Walker planned. "Oh, that's your girlfriend? She's hot!"

I'm so shocked by the teenager's comment that I don't have the time to disguise my choked surprise with a cough.

Laughing, Walker slides his arm around my shoulders and tugs me against him. Looking down, his eyes on mine, he says, "Yeah, she's smokin'."

I slap my hand against his belly. "Walker!"

"What? I'm not gonna lie. You are hot. And you *are* my girlfriend."

"Grandpa says you never lie to your mom or your girl," Danny adds, a nod of his head going along with his imparted wisdom.

"Well, thank you both for the compliment." I smile at Danny. "And that's because *my* grandpa says you always thank someone when they're nice to you."

"Not sure how telling the truth is being nice but whatever," Danny shrugs. "I gotta go stock shelves. See ya later, Mr. Walker."

"See ya, Danny." Walker removes his arm from around me to place his hand on my lower back. "C'mon, let's get home."

I know he doesn't really mean home the way I take it but there's no stopping my visceral reaction to his words. I want to be going *home* with Walker.

Although, with how quickly things between us are moving, I'm beginning to think home isn't a place, it's *him*.

It won't matter where we sleep—his place here, my hotel suite, my house in Baton Rouge—as long as he's there it'll be home.

"You've gone quiet."

"Just thinking."

"You still want to come to my place?"

"Yes, why wouldn't I?"

"Don't know, just wanted to be sure." He grabs my hand and weaves our fingers together. "It's this way," he says with a tug.

"We're not getting a cab?" My stride settles in to match his.

"Nope. It's only a couple of blocks."

The sidewalk is relatively empty and it's an easy stroll in the cold March afternoon air. New York temps are so different from home.

This time in the afternoon at home would be a comfortable low to mid-seventies. Here it's barely hitting fifty.

"You cold?" Walker asks. Letting go of my hand, he slips his arm over my shoulders and pulls me in against his side. "I swear, it's not far. Another few minutes tops."

"Not cold. But I'm definitely not used to the temp being this low in March." I can't help but snuggle closer to his warmth.

"I guess I'll have to get used to that. You don't get snow either, do you?"

"We do...but I wouldn't really say it snows. Not like you're used to."

"This is going to be a mind-trip having the Rogues in a city that doesn't snow." He steers us around a pile of trash. "Going from the heat into the arena is going to be a shock every damn time."

"It is, but we're taking that into account and the areas surrounding the rinks will gradually get cooler from the outside in."

"I haven't even thought about the logistics of getting a rink up and running in the south. Sure, I've played in cities down there, but that's only a couple of days at most." He shakes his head. "This is going to take some adjusting."

"I'm sure you'll be ready by the time we play our first game in the league."

"This is me." He smiles at the doorman who holds the door for us. "Hey, Henry, how're things?"

"Good, sir. You have a package."

Walker's steps falter. "Who's it from?"

"A Mrs. Cantrell. She delivered it personally. Left her number for you to call. She'd like to meet with you as soon as possible, sir." Henry eyes me as though he's not sure he should be saying this in front of me.

"Right. Okay, thanks. This is Oakley—she can come and go whenever she wants. Oak, this is Henry."

"Ma'am." Henry tips his head. "Pleasure."

"Nice to meet you, Henry. How heavy is the package? Can I get it or should I take the grocery bag from Walker and let him take it?"

"Oh, I've already delivered it to the apartment."

"I'm in for the night and not expecting anyone," Walker says.

"I'll call before allowing any surprise visitors up, sir."

"Thanks, Henry. Have a great night."

"You too, sir."

"He seems very attentive," I say as we step into the elevator.

"I'm close with all the doormen, and after I broke things off with you know who and things got a little crazy, I had to make those acquaintances closer."

"Oh." I hadn't thought about the fact Kristina had been in Walker's home.

The thought of her in his space doesn't sit well, although I have no reason to be jealous or angry about it. I hadn't met him then.

"Don't worry, I ditched the bed and bedding when I broke up with her, plus she'd only been her a few times in the years we were together."

"And yet she switched her postal address to here?" I was beginning to think the woman was cracked. Walker's mention of things turning crazy fits right in with this new information.

"That's weird, right?"

I look at him as we reach his floor. "Yeah. Although I think the word you used was crazy."

He places his arm across the open elevator doors and ushers

me out. "Go left," he directs as he follows me. "I'd like to say things went to batshit crazy yesterday."

"What happened yesterday?" I stop and spin around to face him.

"My lack of underwear was because she somehow got hold of my laundry and took scissors to every piece of clothing in it and as I hadn't washed in forever, all my underwear was in there."

"Wow!"

"Yeah, but it gets better. Let's go in so I can tell you about my day."

He wastes no time getting us inside. Together we unload the groceries and by the time he's put the last thing in the fridge, I'm on tenterhooks.

"Tell me, tell me, what happened today? Oh, wait, where's the package Henry brought up. I'm assume Mrs. Cantrell is Laken Cantrell, Jerry's wife?"

"Yeah, when I hunted down Cantrell today, he was with Kristina, at her apartment. But before I could get there they went to Maguire's for a late lunch."

"Maguire's? That's a little public, isn't it? Not to mention on the romantic side."

"Yes, except within a few minutes of my arrival, Mrs. Cantrell and Rafe joined them."

My eyebrows shoot up and my mouth drops open.

"Yeah, that was my reaction too."

"What the hell were they all doing together?" I can understand the Cantrells and Rafe, but Kristina? That doesn't make any kind of sense.

"She tried to say she'd called a meeting to talk about me, but I put that shit to bed quickly then ended up in the back of Mrs. Cantrell's car with her and Rafe. I told them about the pictures, and she assured me the Knights would do the proper paperwork to terminate my contract."

"Laken did?"

"You're on first name bases with Mrs. Cantrell?"

"Ah, yeah, we've met a few times. At fundraisers and such."

"Oh, well, they gave me some information that I can't talk about that convinced me she was on the up and up."

I glance around. "Where's the package?"

"Probably in the office. First door on the left after we came in," Walker directs. "You go find that, I'll get us a drink. We can take a look at what's in it out on the terrace."

"Okay, I'll take cold water."

"You don't want wine?"

I shake my head. "No. Maybe with dinner. But I want a clear head while we hash out the details of our relationship. Well, the details we're going to leak to the media."

"I figure Danny's already told his whole hockey team about my *hot* girlfriend." Walker waggles his eyebrows, making me laugh.

"I like that. No one can say we staged that sighting."

"No. But maybe we should eat out?" He rubs his jaw. "How long are you in town for? What if we eat out tonight, and stay in tomorrow night after my retirement announcement goes out?"

"Will the food be good until then?"

"Yes." He moves toward me. "Tell me exactly what you're thinking about revealing to the press."

"Not much. Just that we've been getting to know each other since you signed the sponsor contract for Rogue sportswear last June."

"But wouldn't you have been here when I was injured? I know I've only known you a day, but you'd have been at my bedside if we were together."

"Yes and no. We weren't *together* then, just friends feeling things out. We talked more after your injury and things developed from there. Until now."

"Okay, okay, I can see how that might work... Friends, then more. Yeah, I like that. And if asked, I can say that you've supported me in my decision to retire."

"Only if asked. Otherwise we don't say anything about it.

And if we're asked when we got together, we can say we decided to make it happen from yesterday. It's why I was at the shoot."

"Right. That makes it sound as though we've put a lot of thought into this and taken things slowly."

"Yes, because you live here and have a lot going on, and I live in Baton Rouge and also have a lot going on. Some of which nobody knows about yet."

He's nodding. "Yeah, this seems plausible and when the announcement about the franchise and my appointment as head coach come out, people will be less likely to think this is a set up."

"They can think it's a set up. I don't care. I'm not going to let rumors get in the way of us or the Rogues."

"Me either." He snags my hand. "Now come here. I want to give you a quick tour of the place."

"Does the tour include your bed?" I wind my arms around his neck.

"If you want. Although now I'm thinking I can show you the highlights then go back to your hotel, pack up your stuff, and have it delivered here while we go out to dinner. Then I can spend all night giving you that bed tour."

WALKER

We're barely in our seats two minutes when the first photographer shows up. Leaning over I speak in Oakley's ear, "Paparazzi across the street."

To her credit she doesn't turn to look. Instead she tilts her face toward me and says, "Then kiss me," before planting her mouth on mine.

It's a short kiss, nothing more than a peck, but it definitely shows we're a couple. "You tip them off?"

"No. The hostess did." Oakley's gaze moves over my shoulder and delight flashes in her eyes before she shoots out of her seat. "Laken!"

Straightening, I get to my feet beside Oakley and wait for our dinner companions to join us.

Turns out the package I got from Mrs. Cantrell was not only my release papers but a dinner invitation for myself and a plus one.

How she knew I had a plus one to bring I don't know; then again, maybe she was just being polite.

I shake Rafe's hand and hide my surprise when Mrs. Cantrell greets me by offering me her cheek.

As I bend down, she whispers, "Call me Laken," before we complete our hellos.

Once everyone is seated, Oakley asks, "How have you been? I haven't seen you since...oh."

"Yes. Gerald's funeral."

"I'm so sorry."

"Don't be. He's better off now. The cancer hit hard, and at the end it was a mercy for him to go." Laken's mouth tips up in a sad smile. "And he did some things before he went that mean I won't have to remain where I am."

Oakley leans closer to Laken. "He did it? He talked with Pa about what he was thinking of doing. They even drew up a plan with the steps he'd need to take but I wasn't sure, especially with Jerry at the helm of..." Her words trail off when Laken shakes her head.

"He did. And until now, it's been kept quiet."

"Jerry doesn't know, does he?" Oakley asks, a smirk curving her lips. "Because he'd be kicking up a stink if he did."

"Let's just say things are going to get stinky around New York in the next few weeks." Laken's smile is all pleasure now.

"What do you ladies want to drink?" Rafe asks.

I'm not sure if the change in subject is on purpose or not, because within a few seconds a waiter appears beside our table.

"Oh, I'll have a gin and tonic," Laken says before turning to our waiter. "Can you ask the barman to make it in a tall glass, please."

"Yes, ma'am."

"I'll take a glass of chardonnay," Oakley orders.

"Water for me," I say as Rafe says, "Scotch, rocks."

Everyone looks me. I know what they're thinking, and I can't really blame them for their surprise. So once the waiter leaves to fill our orders, I explain.

"I haven't had a drop of alcohol since before the season started, and I might not be playing but it's not the end of the season yet." I shrug.

Oakley opens her mouth then snaps it closed. "Before the waiter returns, I have to ask, does Walker need to be concerned about what's about to happen with Jerry?"

I'm confused by her question. I don't know how the situation between Cantrell, his wife, or the Knights would affect me.

Rafe is shaking his head but it's Laken who answers.

"No. Definitely not." Her eyes flick to me before returning to Oakley. "I'll be filing for divorce next week. Until then the true ownership of the Knights will remain secret, and Rafe will continue to do the job he was hired to do."

"So Walker's in the clear?"

"Yes. He just has to pick up anything he has left at the arena," Rafe confirms.

"I've got nothing there. Gannon collected the last of my personal stuff months ago."

"Then yes, you're in the clear." Rafe's mouth kicks up on one end. "Although I'm not sure you're out of the firing line of your ex."

"What? Why?"

"She doesn't strike me as the type to give up easily."

"Then she'll see just how much of a prick I can be when necessary."

Rafe's eyes move to Oakley then back to me. "Are you going to use what—"

"I gave them to him so he could."

I glance at Oakley. "I didn't tell them where I got them from."

She waves her hand, dismissing my concern. "It's fine. Laken and Rafe can know I'm the one who initiated the investigation that uncovered the affair."

"How do you know I told them about that?"

Oakley's gaze meets mine. "Because you're you and there's no way you wouldn't reveal who else was in those pictures when it became obvious Laken was making moves to get out."

"Huh." I fold my arms over my chest. "You're far too smart."

She grins at me then leans in to press her lips to mine. "You like my smarts."

Grinning against her mouth, I say, "I like a lot of your things."

"Should we leave you two alone?" Rafe asks, humor lacing his words.

"Sorry, sorry." Oakley moves back into her seat properly. "This part of our relationship is new. We've been building to this for months now, and we're keen to move things forward."

"Well, now that you're not tied to New York, Walker, you'll be able to see each other more," Laken offers.

"Yes. That's the plan," I answer.

The waiter returns with our drinks and asks, "Ready to order?"

None of us has even glanced at the menu but before we can comment, a man in chef's whites walks up to our table.

"Laken, lovely to see you." He leans over and kisses both her cheeks. "Will you allow me to choose your meals for tonight?"

"I'm fine with that." Laken looks at us in turn. "I can vouch for Chef Kegan's talents. He will not disappoint."

"Sure, I'm game." I glance at Oakley to see her nodding.

"Yes. Me too."

"Raff?" Chef Kegan arches a brow.

"Cook me what you want, little brother," Rafe answers with a grin.

"Wait." Oakley's gaze bounces between the two men. "You're brothers?"

"Did the name of the restaurant not give it away?" Rafe asks.

"But it's...oh. Your last name is Rafferty?"

"No. My first name, but shithead here decided it would be funny to name this place after me. Raff is what my family calls me. Hence, Raff's."

"I never made the connection." I shake my head. "And I've been eating here for years."

"We try not to make the connection. Or at least we don't

advertise it," Kegan explains. Then he rubs his hands together. "All right. I'll be back with your first course shortly."

When he's gone, Oakley says, "You look nothing alike."

"We're adopted. All seven of us."

"There are seven of you? Your poor mother."

"There's nothing poor about my mother. She could have been a drill sergeant. Hell, she basically was. Not one of us boys stepped out of line when we were younger and if she finds out we do now, she isn't above an ear twist to pull us back in."

Rafe is chuckling and I feel a pang of regret. I miss having that relationship with my mother. She might not have been as formidable as Rafe's mother sounds but she still knew how to pull me and Shelby into line.

"You okay?" Oakley whispers in my ear.

"Yeah, just feeling nostalgic."

"Ah, right. Well, I'm feeling envious. I didn't have any relationship with my mother. I don't remember the woman. And my father was out of my life when I was three."

She looks stricken for a second then shakes her head.

"I don't know why I told you that here."

I slip my arm around her and pulling her close, drop a kiss on her temple. "You can tell me anything any time."

Smiling up at me, she mouths 'thank you' before turning to our companions. "When are you going to visit me in Baton Rouge, Laken?"

"I'll be busy for the next few months. Maybe after the season is over?"

"Yes. Let's plan that."

"Does your grandfather still head north for the summer?" Laken asks and I realize these two know each other more than Oakley let on.

Rafe and I sit in silence and let the women talk for a few minutes. He's to the right of me and I find it hard to see him clearly without facing him head on.

And I don't want to be caught staring but I'm curious about his and Laken's relationship.

In the car earlier they gave me the impression that they have a longstanding connection and having them both join us for dinner only confirms it.

I want to ask how long they've known each other. Rafe has been GM for the Knights since before Gerald Senior died. I think it was five years before. Possibly more.

"Oh, here comes Kegan," Laken says.

"All right. These aren't on the menu yet. I'm thinking of adding them, so I want you to give me your honest opinion when you're done."

He places a platter of small bite size...I have no idea what, in the middle of the table.

"Are these those veggie tower things you served at Mom's last Christmas," Rafe asks, leaning over for a closer look.

"Yes. But with a twist." Kegan puts his hand on his brother's shoulder. "See if you can tell me what that twist is."

"I love it when you test your new recipes on us." Laken looks up at Kegan. "I'm going to assume this is an improvement over the others."

"I think so but what would I know?" He shrugs then leans over, dropping his voice so only our table can hear him. "At last count there were ten out front and Mica said when he took his break out back, there were a few at the end of the alley, but he couldn't be sure how many."

"Thanks for the heads up. We'll be going out the front door." Oakley looks at me. "We may have been keeping our friendship on the down low but that's no longer the case."

"Okay, but let me know if there is anything you need me or my staff to do to make your evening enjoyable."

"Get back in that kitchen and cook me the rest of my meal," Oakley demands with a smile and wink to soften it.

Kegan chuckles as he reaches for Oakley's hand and bows his head over it. "As you command, my lady."

Before he can put his lips on her skin, I'm putting my hand on top of hers. "Hey. Keep your lips to yourself."

For a second the table is silent, then Oakley laughs, snapping everyone else out of the moment.

"Right. Well, yet again the fair maiden is snatched up before I can make my move." Kegan looks at his brother. "It seems to be the way of the King men."

I'm not sure what passes between them in that moment but Rafe moves his gaze to Laken for a split second.

It confirms my thoughts that Rafe and Laken have a long-time friendship. I can't remember when she married Cantrell, but I know it wasn't that long before Gerald Senior died. Maybe four years.

"Dig in. I'll be back with another course in about fifteen minutes."

Kegan leaves us, the lull in conversation hanging over the table, but it's not uncomfortable. Finally Laken breaks the silence by picking up one of the small bites using her fingers.

"Sorry. Can't wait. They were absolutely delicious last time and Kegan says these are better so..." She shrugs and shoves the whole thing in her mouth.

A second later her eyes close with a soft moan.

"Oh, I'm not waiting if that's the reaction." Oakley follows Laken's example and picks up a bite using her fingers then pops it into her mouth.

Hand over her lips, she makes a sound that reminds me of one she makes when she's close to orgasm, and my pants grow tight. "Oak," I murmur.

She reaches out for another bite and brings it to my mouth. "Here. You have to try this."

As soon as I open my mouth to protest, she shoves the food inside. Left with no choice but to eat, I close my lips, snagging the tips of her fingers when I do.

For a moment we remain like that, Oakley's fingertips in my mouth and our eyes locked. Then the flavors of the food register and I can't stop the sound of pleasure that rumbles in my chest.

Smiling, Oakley pulls her hand away. "See?"

Swallowing, I reach out for another bite. "Oh yeah, but then I've never had anything here that wasn't delicious."

"Me either, but I think Kegan has outdone himself with these," Laken adds. Turning to Rafe, she asks, "You're not eating?"

"You know I like seeing other people enjoying my brother's food. But yes, I'll have one."

Rafe is true to his word. He has one. Then he sits back and watches the rest of us devour every last morsel while sipping his scotch.

"So how long have you two known each other?" he asks, eyes on me.

Before I can take a sip of water to clear my throat, Oakley takes the lead.

"Eight months?" she arches an eyebrow my way. "No, wait, twelve. It was before you signed on to be the face of our new elite collection."

"Yeah, you wanted to see me in person before you made the final offer." I smirk.

It's all bullshit. We didn't even speak on the phone, but we've laid out how it could have gone and that's the story we're selling to everyone, including the two people across from us.

Oakley leans her elbow on the table and looks at me with soft eyes. "We hit it off but Walker was in the middle of the season, and I was launching last year's summer lines so we kept missing each other a lot of the time."

"Yeah, it was a lot of ships passing in the night for the first few months. Then when I was injured..."

"We—"

"You!"

"Yes, me." Oakley smiles. "I decided he should concentrate on recovery. We still stayed in contact."

"She's been instrumental in keeping me sane while I made a decision about my future." I slide my hand over her thigh. "I'd probably still be denying the situation if it weren't for her."

Those last words are true. If it wasn't for her lifeline, for the job and future she's offering me, I'd be wallowing in the dark in my apartment.

"Nonsense." She sits straight and puts her hand over mine. "You don't need me to make the tough decisions."

"No. I don't. But I'm grateful to have you there to support me."

We're laying it on a bit thick, but we talked about it before leaving home. We need everyone—including ourselves—to believe our relationship, the closeness of it, has been months in the making.

It's the only way others will accept the depth of our connection. Because the more time I spend with Oakley, the deeper I fall and she's right behind me. I can't believe it's not obvious to everyone around us that we're falling in love.

Fuck.

I think I'm already there.

"Well, I wish you both the very best in the future." Laken holds up her gin and tonic. "To relationships, may they be strong, devoted, and everything you've ever dreamed of."

Raising my water, I can't help notice the clench in Rafe's jaw. And the words he mutters next explains his tension. "And may the toxic ones be removed from our lives sooner than later."

"Oh, I'll toast to that." Oakley side-eyes me. "Some of us need a little house cleaning in that department."

"Hey, you know I've done my best there."

She pats my hand where it rests on her leg. "I do. But sometimes we need to use a little more force to scrub the scum away."

I laugh. I can't help it. The second my brain registers her words, images of Oakley dressed in a hazmat suit with industrial cleaning supplies surrounding her came to mind.

"Why are you laughing?" She eyes me quizzically.

"I can see you decked out for a biohazard event in my head."

"Well, I have to admit, she is a biohazard."

"Are you referring to Kristina?" Laken leans forward. "Because if so, I'm got some intel that you should have before it gets out."

"Oh?" Oakley leans in. "Do tell."

"She's apparently pregnant."

"What?" I sputter, the water I just sipped spraying into my hand.

Laken nods, her eyes on me. "I hear she was looking to pin that on you."

"Ha! I haven't touched the woman in over a year. Not since I laid eyes on Oak."

It's not a lie. I haven't been with Kristina in a physical way since last season. I can't even remember when exactly, but I know it's been over a year.

"Ah, how sweet." Laken's gaze moves to Oakley. "I'm so glad you found a man who appreciates you for who you are."

Deciding the evening needs an injection of humor, I say, "Are you kidding? I always wanted a sugar mamma."

It takes a second for them to realize I'm joking, but once they do the laughter lasts a while.

And it's the perfect start to the rest of our meal. Which is full of great conversation and the most divine food I've ever tasted.

OAKLEY

"Thanks for the ride." I lean in to hug Laken and whisper, "Call if you need anything."

She holds on a little tighter. "I will. I hope I won't have to, but I will. I'm over not asking for help. Promise."

I let her go and offer my hand to Rafe. "It was a pleasure to meet you, and let me thank you for the lovely meal because I'm sure it wouldn't have been anywhere near as delicious if I hadn't been dining with the chef's brother."

"Oh, I wouldn't bet on that. The menu at Raff's is always above par." He adds a smile to his handshake and I have to wonder if he'll be so friendly when he finds out about the Rogues.

"Well, I suppose it would have to be, but nothing beats personalized service from the chef himself." Walker slips his arm around my waist. "We should do this again."

"Yes. Next time you're in New York." Laken puts her hand on Rafe's arm. "We should get going. I have to be up early to meet with the lawyers."

"I told you I'd go with you."

She's shaking her head. "Not this time. I need to take this first step on my own."

I don't know what's going on with these two but I'm glad my

friend has someone in her corner. I'm ashamed to admit after Gerald Senior died, I let my friendship with Laken slip. I should have made more of an effort to stay in contact.

"I'll call you next week," I say to Laken. "We can make time to chat over a glass of wine."

I don't need to elaborate to let her know I'll be her sounding board or shoulder or soldier. I know she's in for a rough few months, and I'll do my best to support her.

"I'd like that. But I'm not sure how much time I'll have—"

"I'll make sure you have time." Rafe's words are made of steel.

"On that note." Laken gives me another smile and quick hug. "We really need to go."

We stand on the sidewalk outside Walker's apartment and wait for them to get back in Laken's SUV.

The driver closes the door behind them before turning to us, "Get in out of the cold."

I grin, recognizing Arthur from trips I took with Pa to visit Gerald Senior. It's a reminder that I should fill Walker in on the history between my family and the Cantrells.

"Goodnight, Arthur, drive safe."

"Always, Miss Annie."

I laugh at the nickname from my childhood and do as he says.

Looking up at Walker, I say, "C'mon, it is cold out here. Especially for this thin-blooded woman."

He tightens his hold around my waist and ushers me toward the building. Before we reach it, Henry steps out and holds the door open.

"Evening."

"Henry." Walker urges me ahead of him. "We're in for the night for real this time."

Henry chuckles. "Okay, sir. I'll be sure you're not disturbed."

"Did my luggage arrive?" I ask.

"Yes, ma'am, it's been delivered to Mr. Alcott's."

"Thank you, Henry. Have a good night," I say as we head for the elevator.

Even though I know I have to explain a few things to Walker and I'm sure he has questions, we're quiet on the ride up to his apartment.

There's a buzz vibrating over my skin and sliding through my veins. I know what it is.

The low simmer of arousal.

The sweet heat of anticipation.

Dinner was a lesson in sexual restraint.

So many times I wanted to kiss him. Wanted to put my hands on him, tangle my fingers in his hair, give in to the lust I could see in his eyes every time he glanced at me.

Every time he put his hand on my thigh, his mouth on mine, I wanted to launch out of my seat and drag him from the restaurant.

I've never had to work to control my sexual urges the way I have in the last few hours. It makes me wonder if what we have is only sex.

But then I think about the way he takes care of me in small ways, like wrapping his arm around me while we're out in the cold air. Or when he checks to make sure I'm not flashing myself to anyone who cares to look in my hotel suite.

We might be dealing with instant lust but it's not the only thing between us. I can't explain it, don't want to examine it, and I certainly don't want to walk away from it.

No, no matter what happens between us, if we make a personal and professional relationship work or not, I'm not walking away.

All I want to do is get closer. And I know if I touch him before we get inside his apartment, I'll end up on my knees in front of him.

I want to put my mouth on him. I want to weaken his knees. I want to take everything he has to give.

My body is vibrating from head to toe as we leave the elevator and make our way to his place. Clenching my hands, I wait for him to unlock the door with barely concealed impatience.

And the second Walker closes the door behind us, I pounce.

Catching him by surprise, I manage to shove him back against the wall and kiss him.

I kiss him hard.

I kiss him deep.

I kiss him until we're both breathless.

Tearing my mouth from his, I suck in great big drafts of air.

"Whoa." He licks his lips. "What brought that on?"

Tilting my head I ask, "I need a reason to kiss us both stupid?"

Laughing, he tugs me back to him and proves I'm not the only one good at kissing us stupid.

And as much as I love kissing him—him kissing me—I want something else.

Pulling back, I reach down and grab a handful of my sheath dress. It's loose and only mid-thigh length, so it takes no effort at all to pull it up and over my head.

Walker chokes on a sucked-in breath and I can't stop the curl of my lips.

The demi bra I'm wearing is sheer, and really, I'd have more coverage wearing plastic wrap. My thong panties match, and I know he can see how wet I am for him.

"Oak," he says my name on a sigh, and I shiver as the nickname washes over me. "Come—"

I dodge his hand and drop to my knees. Before he can argue, I've got the button and zipper on his slacks open and my hand curled around his hardening shaft.

"Oakley." When he reaches for me again, I brush his hands away.

"No. I want to do this. Here. Now."

I can't explain the depth of my need to do this for him. I've given head before, even enjoyed it, but the desire scraping through me is raw and urgent and unlike any I've felt before.

After studying me for long seconds, he gives a nod and I wrap my lips around the plump tip of his cock.

Not that I need his permission to suck him off. I think we've proven over the last day that neither of us can deny the other.

I start slow, a gentle pull, a slow sweep of my tongue around the head then down the shaft.

He pulses and jumps against my tongue, and I grip the base of his length tighter. Adding my other hand, I slide it into his pants and cup his balls.

They're already tucked up in his groin, the skin puckered tight, and I smile at the grumble of pleasure that comes from him when I lightly graze my nails over them.

"Oakley," he puffs, his breath stuttering when I put my lips to his crown. But that's nothing compared to the guttural curse that follows when I suck him deep. "Fuck!"

His fingers tangle in my hair, the tug no more than a mild sting, but it sends a shiver of delight down my spine.

I work him slowly, not too much pressure, just enough. I don't want him going off too soon. I want us both to enjoy this.

"Oak. Jesus, woman, you're gonna make me come."

His grip on my head tightens, the sting not so pleasurable now but it's the kind of pain that melds with the lust pinging across my nerves and turns into pleasure.

"Not in your mouth." He reaches down, tries to get his hands under my arms but I clamp them close to my sides and suck him harder, work my hand on his shaft faster. "Fuck. Fuck. Fuck."

If I didn't have a mouth full of his dick I'd laugh. His fingers go back to my hair and with a hard yank that brings tears to my eyes he finally achieves his objective.

"Dammit, Oakley!" He's breathing hard, his chest heaving, air sawing in and out of his mouth as though he's been under water too long.

Smiling up at him I ask, "You didn't like that?"

"Fuck. Get up." His voice is tight, his jaw the same. "I'm not fucking your face in the goddamn foyer."

I laugh and push to my feet. Taking a step back I reach out a hand. "How about fucking my face in your bedroom?"

Continuing to walk backward, I keep my eyes on his until he pushes off the wall and follows.

Once he places his hand in mine, I glance around to orient myself. The place looks different in the dark and the tour he gave me earlier didn't include light switches.

Not that the room is completely dark. The wall of windows in the living room offers enough illumination to find the way.

"You should turn around before you trip in those heels." Walker has a hand fisted in the side of his pants keeping them up, and I think about telling him to strip them off but I like the idea of him being fully clothed while I'm not.

"I can kick them off—"

"No. I want you to leave them on. I've been fantasizing about them since you walked out of the hotel bedroom in them earlier."

I smile. "As you wish."

He cocks his head and grins at me. "Is this a Walker gets three wishes night?"

"If it was, what would you wish for?" I'm still moving backward, my hand in his, and I feel him push on our hold, a subtle direction indicator I'm happy to follow.

"I get three?"

I shrug. "Sure." Although, let's be honest, I'll give him as many as he wants.

"Hmm... Okay, number one, you in those heels bent over the bed while I fuck you from behind."

A shudder rolls through me, drawing a smile from him.

"Two, your legs up over my shoulders, your heels beside my head."

His words paint clear images in my head, and I know my thong is completely soaked through. "One more," I say, my voice breathy with lust.

"I can't decide if I want you crouching over my face, your heels planting on the bed next to my ears or your legs around my waist, those spikes digging into my ass while I fuck you hard."

The hallway to his bedroom is darker than the living room

and I slow until I'm sure I'm heading straight. But truly, his words have turned my body sluggish, the molten heat in my veins making my legs wobble in my shoes.

The knowing smirk on his lips comes closer and the next thing I know he's backed me up against his closed bedroom door.

"I'm going to fuck you all night in those shoes." His warm breath fans out over my jaw. "But first, you're going to get on your knees again and finish what you started."

"Here?" I'm already bending my knees, but he stops me.

"No." He reaches behind me and opens the door, making me stumble back a step. "Over there."

I look over my shoulder to where he's pointing. It's the floor to ceiling windows his king-sized bed faces. "Oh."

"Yeah, right there, your back to the glass, so I can enjoy the view."

He wants to look at the city? Before I can voice the question, he's crowding close.

"I'm not talking about what's outside, Oakley." He grips my chin and turns me to look at him. When he's got my full attention, he says, "I'm talking about our reflection."

Using his grip on my jaw he turns me to look at the window again. That's when I see what he's talking about.

I can already see us, not clearly, but we're there and if we were closer…the thrill that shoots through me is electrifying.

Walker leans in, his lips brushing my ear, and whispers, "But I'm not going to come down your throat. I'm going to pull you up and spin you around, press your hands to the glass and fuck you against it."

I'm not sure if it's all the dirty talk, the images rolling through my head, or the man himself, but I'm so close to coming right now it's ridiculous.

If I wasn't experiencing it, I'd call bullshit.

Swallowing, I roll my lips between my teeth before licking them. "Okay."

The word is breathy, barely audible, but he hears it, feels it in the tremble of my body.

"God, Oak, you're so fucking sexy, you do me in."

Ha! Like he can talk. He's got me riding the edge with words and I'm frightened the second I take a step, the moment my legs move, the wet crotch of my thong is going to rub my clit and take me to my knees.

But my knees are where I want to be, where Walker wants me, so with teeth clamped tight, fists clenched at my sides, I step away from him and head for the window.

Once there, relief flows over me and I sink to the floor, my back to the window, and tip my chin up and lock my gaze on his.

I know he's a man of his word, and I have no doubt the next little while is going to be the hottest sexual experience of my life.

With each step he takes toward me, my breath shortens and sweat slicks my skin. The thrum between my legs becomes so intense I have to widen my knees or risk coming without him touching me.

He's eyeing me, his gaze probing and concerned. "You okay?"

I nod, not sure I can manage words.

Then a smile tips up one side of his mouth, and he says, "You're so close."

Another nod is all he gets.

"Damn. That's so fucking hot. I've barely touched you."

"You've been touching me all night," I argue.

He's grinning now. "So I have. But I honestly thought I was the only one affected by it."

"No."

"Oakley, I know I just painted a picture for us, but I have to say I don't think I can do it. Not without losing it the second I stick my cock between your lips and I find myself wanting to fill your pussy so badly I'm shaking."

"Oh."

"And I don't want it against the windows. I want you in my

bed. I want to drive you so deep into the mattress, the imprint of you stays there forever."

I lick my lips. Fuck, this man knows how to paint a picture. I'm so weak with desire, I'm not sure I can get up without his help.

Raising my hand, I wait for him to thread our fingers together and tug me to my feet before saying, "Take me to bed, Walker."

He smiles down at me. "It'll be fast and furious this first time."

I nod. I'm okay with that. More than okay with that. I'm like a grenade with the pin pulled, seconds away from exploding.

"And as much as I love those heels and tiny strips of lace, I want you naked, want to be skin to skin, head to toe the first time I have you in my bed."

Without letting go of his hand, I slip out of my shoes and use my other hand to push my panties down. The bra isn't as easy, and he lets go so I can remove it while he discards his own clothes.

I don't think I'll ever get over how good he looks naked. The muscles he's spent years honing draw my eyes and hands, but the second my fingertips touch his skin, he moves.

His hands grip my waist, and he lifts me off the floor. In two strides he's beside the bed and tossing me onto it.

I can't help the laughter that bubbles up my throat. The sound of my joy fills the room, surrounds us.

It fizzes and pops in my veins like the finest champagne.

And just like that high priced liquid, Walker is decadent and makes my head spin.

WALKER

I lower myself on top of Oakley. Her legs immediately part to make room for mine and my cock fits snug up against her hot pussy.

Resting on my elbows I look down at her. I want to etch every second of our time together in my memory so I can pull it out whenever we're apart.

I don't know what will happen in the next few weeks, don't know if we'll have to be away from each other as we sort through both our futures.

She needs to concentrate on the Rogues announcement and I have to deal with my retirement.

Then there's the logistics of where we live, the move I need to make to join her down south.

"Walker?" Her hand cups my jaw and I lean into it.

I smile. "You take my breath away and it's not because you're naked under me."

She returns my smile and moves her hand up the side of my face until her fingers are in my hair. With a little pressure she pulls me down. "Kiss me."

She doesn't need to ask. My mouth is already aiming for hers.

I take my time, press lightly, angle my head, and press a bit harder. It's nothing like the kisses we've shared since we got inside the front door.

This is sweet and tender and says far more than either of us is willing to voice yet.

I can't see my life without this woman in it. I can't imagine spending a night without her in my bed.

It's only the second night we've spent together, and I know I never want to sleep apart again. And I'm not just talking about sex.

I want her head on the pillow next to mine. I want her scent on the sheets. Hell, I want our clothes in the same closet and dresser. I want her girly stuff cluttering the counters in the bathroom.

I want my ring on her finger.

Pulling back, I stare into her eyes and try to convey everything I'm feeling. Neither of us is ready for where my head and heart are going.

I can't believe I'm even thinking of forever when less than forty-eight hours ago we hadn't met.

"Oakley." I swallow. "I..."

Her smile is sweet and knowing and without saying a word I know she gets it, understands what's going through my head.

"One day at a time."

Her words are soft, a whisper in the night between us, and I want to argue, want to have that ring on her finger as soon as possible but I know we've got other stuff to deal with.

If I had those wishes we joked about earlier, I'd use one to wish the world away. To wish all the complications and obstacles we're bound to face away too.

"One day at a time," I say before pressing my mouth to hers.

This kiss is deeper, wetter, and as each second ticks by, turns more carnal. By the time I pull back to drag in a breath, we're both panting and our hips are rocking together.

It takes no effort, no stumbling moves or awkward directions to slip my cock into her. To push in deep and take all she is, give all I am.

"Walker." She murmurs my name against my jaw and I'm helpless to deny her anything.

The way she sounds when she calls to me while I'm buried inside her is the most magnificent sound I've ever heard, and I've heard the buzzer at the end of a winning game for the Cup.

I don't know if it's because I'm at a crossroads or if it's just Oakley, but I've never felt anything like the euphoria I feel when I'm with her.

How do you fall in love in one day?

How do you connect with someone so deeply, so completely, within hours of meeting?

How does something so new feel so familiar, so right?

I can't answer any of those questions except to say it can happen. I'm feeling it, living it, falling deep into it in a way I never dreamed existed.

"We will make this work." It's a promise, a demand, a vow.

"We will."

Her agreement should soothe me, should ease the anxiety thrumming through me when I think about letting her out of this bed.

"I know I said fast and furious but..."

"Slow and easy works too."

"It all works."

I'm talking about more than the physical between us. Tonight at dinner, sitting beside her, talking with her and our companions, didn't feel like the first time.

Nothing with Oakley feels like the first time.

"How long will it take you to pack up your life here?" she asks.

"I'll leave it all behind." I don't care about any of it. I don't care what happens to it.

Laughing, she brushes her hand down over my head to my neck. She grips me, her hold firm, and locks her gaze with mine.

"You will not. We'll take a couple of days to sort things then head to Baton Rouge. Together."

"It might all blow up in our faces tomorrow." I can't believe I'm voicing the fear. Except it's been playing in the back of my mind all night.

Once we stepped out in public, we opened up our little bubble, and I know there will be talk. Add in the announcement going out to the media tomorrow about my retirement and we're in for a lot of attention.

Attention we've avoided because we've been behind closed doors.

Not to mention this is all new.

So new this time two days ago we hadn't met.

"Walker." The snap in her voice pulls me from my head. "We'll deal with whatever happens."

"Together."

"Together." Her hands trail down my back where she digs her fingers into my ass. "Now get going with the slow and easy or fast and furious."

She's grinning, her eyes sparkling and I know everything will be okay. We'll have shit to handle but we'll handle it.

Together.

I move slowly, softly, smoothly. Gliding my cock in and out with gentle slides of hard through soft. It's an easy rock of my hips against hers.

And the whole time our gazes stay locked. In her eyes I see my future, a life I never dreamed of before meeting her.

I want to tell her I love her but I know it's too soon to utter those words. But I can show her. I can make her feel them with every breath she takes for the rest of the night.

And as much as she wanted to worship me when we got home, as much as I wanted to let her, I want to worship her more.

Before the sun comes up and we have to deal with the world outside, she'll be in no doubt I'm all in.

Picking up the pace, I push harder, faster, and take us up to the peak we were both so close to before I let my emotions and fear get in our way.

There will be time to indulge those later. After I've given her so much pleasure, she's breathless and limp and falling asleep in my arms.

Breaking eye contact, I lower my head and kiss her jaw, her cheek, her lips. It's the last that snags me. Catches me in the lush heat of her mouth and keeps me there.

She gives as well as takes, and in seconds we've gone from slow and easy to fast and furious.

The tension in her body under me reveals her need and the tingle and pull of my balls tucking up speaks of mine.

I keep my mouth on hers, lips and tongue and teeth; we sip and stroke and nip. All the while I'm driving my cock into her in deep hard plunges of advance and retreat.

Heat and pleasure and gasps and moans surround us. The scent of our sex fills my nose and the slap of our bodies coming together fills my ears.

It's a symphony of lust and love and I know I'm not the only one feeling that way.

I don't know how much longer I can hold off saying the words. They're burning my tongue. Pounding in my brain to match the pounding of my pulse in my veins.

Every part of me beats a rhythm as old as time, one I've never heard or felt before. One I can't ignore.

And as Oakley tips over the peak and her body grips mine and takes me with her, I'm helpless to keep the words inside.

Burying my face in the curve of her throat, I utter words I've never spoken to any other woman. And never will.

"I love you."

Clouds have moved in and stolen the light of the moon, leaving the bedroom in darkness.

I want to turn on the light so I can watch Oakley sleep. Except I don't want to wake her. I'm not ready to hear what she has to say about the words I spoke into her skin.

They're true, as fucking bizarre as it is to know that after less than two days together.

I have no doubt she heard me. I felt her stiffen under me, in my arms. Her silence concerned me until I looked into her eyes and saw the moisture filling them.

The emotion in her gaze was breath stealing and I found it hard to keep looking at her.

I'd been overwhelmed and out of control and I'd seen the same in her eyes so I'd given us both a reprieve by getting up and heading into the bathroom to get a cloth to clean up.

She let me take care of her and after I tossed the face cloth toward the bathroom and pulled her into my arms, I tucked her head beneath my chin.

It didn't take long for her to drift off to sleep. And the soft weight of her at my side, the way she uses my shoulder as a pillow, has me breathing easy even if I still can't find the peace of sleep.

Tomorrow will bring who knows what and I know I can't predict or control it in any way. Except after the drama of the media frenzy after my injury I have no desire to relive that kind of attention.

Sighing, I snuggle Oakley closer to me. I need to rest if I'm going to be able to stand beside her for what will no doubt be some trying weeks ahead.

The least of which will be my retirement announcement.

I can't decide if the franchise announcement or my head coach role will cause the bigger stir.

"You can't solve all our problems when we don't know what they are." Oakley's sleepy voice rumbles against my chest.

"I thought you were asleep."

"I was."

"Sorry. Didn't mean to wake you."

She laughs drowsily. "You didn't. I have to pee."

"Oh." I lift my arm and let her up.

"Back in a minute."

She's just a shadow as she rolls out of bed and pads across the room. I'm surprised and yet not when she doesn't bother shutting the bathroom door.

We're so comfortable with each other that the need for closed doors while taking care of a nature call isn't necessary.

Relief flows through me. Any concern I had about whispering I love you is gone because without words she's just told me she's on the same page.

The level of trust and acceptance the act of leaving the door open as she takes care of such a personal need is something you don't give a two-night stand.

I know that's not what we are, not after she orchestrated the photographers getting their pictures of us together. If she planned to ditch me when she went back home, she wouldn't have done that.

Hell, what the fuck am I thinking?

She'd never have gotten into bed with me after offering me the job of head coach if her plan was to walk away after our time together here.

Scrubbing a hand over my face, I try to clear my head.

I'm not used to the emotional upheaval I've gone through in recent months, the last few days especially.

What with meeting Oakley and admitting my playing career is over.

"Hey." Oakley crawls into bed and lays on top of me. "What's wrong?"

"Just my brain freaking out."

"Over what you said?" I feel her stiffen above me and I wrap my arms around her.

"No. Yes. Fuck. There's so much going on in my head, but I meant what I said."

"Well, that's good, because no take-backs."

I grin. "Oh?"

"You gave those words to me so they're mine now and I'm keeping them."

"You want them?"

"Yes." She leans down and presses her mouth to mine. "And I know it's crazy—we just met—but I love you too, Walker."

Air rushes from my chest and an ache I wasn't aware of disappears. "Okay. Good. Good. Okay."

She laughs, her breasts jiggling against my chest. "Can you sleep now? We have a lot to deal with in the morning."

"Yeah, we do. I wish I knew what it was that we needed to deal with."

"We do. Your statement will be released and no doubt our relationship will be splashed across the internet before that."

"Which do you think will garner more attention?"

"Your retirement."

"Yeah? You don't think me dating the CEO of Rogue sportswear is a big deal?"

"Oh, it's the biggest deal but I think your retirement will be what gets the most attention because you've been in the news for months. Now they'll have what they've been searching for."

"What?"

"When you'll be getting back on the ice."

"I need to tell you something." I don't know when I made the decision to tell her, but I know I can't go to sleep tonight until I have. "I'm not retiring because of my knees."

"Okay," she drags the word out.

"You know I had a mild concussion."

"Yes."

"Well, the hit wasn't enough to scramble my brain completely or even forever, but it did cause damage to my right eye."

"What?" she pushes up, but I hold her down.

"I've lost peripheral vision on the right."

"You lost your sight?" Now she pushing against me and trying harder to sit up. "What the fuck, Walker?"

"I'm fine. It's fine. Well, it's not but it hasn't improved; they don't know if it will."

"Whoa, whoa, whoa, let me up. I need the light on."

I let her go and reach over to switch on the beside lamp.

She's looking at me in horror and all I want to do is reassure her I'm okay. "I'm fine, Oakley. I can see. And the loss is only a small amount but it's enough to stop me from being able to see anyone on that side of me. I wouldn't see a puck or a hit coming until it was too late."

"Oh, Walker." The tears in her eyes spill over.

Holding out a hand I say, "Come here." Pulling her in, I hold her close and let her cry. "I haven't told anyone the exact reason I'm calling it. Drake knows the most, but he thinks it's my knees, not my sight."

She sniffles into my neck. "Does he know about your sight at all?"

"Yes."

"Are you going to reveal why you're retiring in your announcement?"

"I wasn't going to but I'm wondering now if I should."

"Does anyone really need to know? It doesn't seem to be something you have to reveal."

I shrug. "I've never thought about it. We went bare bones on the announcement. Hell, we didn't even tell the Knights why I was retiring, just that it was due to the injuries I received on ice."

"Leave it that way. No one needs to know. I won't tell anyone."

"I'll need to tell Blake if only so we can work together without difficulty."

"I haven't noticed anything. Not once did I suspect you had a vision issue."

"It's not obvious; it would be during a game though."

"I'll leave it to you who you tell. Just let me know so I'm aware."

"I think I should tell the whole Rogues org, from the players to the front office to the arena staff."

"Do you want to tell the public? Or leave it to naturally filter out?"

"How about we worry about it after the franchise announcement."

"We can do that."

"Okay. Now we should get some sleep." I reach over and tap my phone. "Shit. It's five-fifteen."

"Almost time to get up." Oakley snuggles in as I slide back down the bed with her in my arms.

She's asleep again in seconds and this time instead of staying awake and overthinking everything I'm right behind her.

OAKLEY

Shrieking wakes me.

One minute I'm dead to the world and the next I'm standing beside the bed, naked, my head whipping back and forth as I search for the source of the ear-piercing noise.

"Fuck!" Walker rolls off the other side of the bed and stumbles around before snatching his briefs from last night off the floor. "Stay—"

His words are cut off when the door flies open, crashing into the wall, and a woman barrels in. "I forgot the code. I can't turn it off. You keep changing...the...code..." her words trail off as her eyes lock on me. "*Oh*."

"Fuck, Shel." Walker stalks over to me and tugs a shirt over my head. "What the hell are you doing here?"

"Um, I, um..."

The silence left in the wake of her inability to find words catches my attention. "It stopped."

"Huh?" Walker helps me get my arms through the sleeves of one of his t-shirts.

"The alarm. I'm assuming that's what that noise was. It's stopped."

"Good, I thought—" His words are cut off by the ring of his phone. "Fucking hell. That'll be the security company."

"I'll wait out—" The lethal look Walker sends his sister's way has her scurrying from the room, yanking the door shut behind her.

I can't help the chuckle that slips out. This morning's wake up isn't as nice as yesterday's but I don't wish I was anywhere else. Even if I'm about to meet Walker's sister for the first time.

I know about her. The PI was thorough in his research on Walker and a full report was compiled about Shelby Alcott because of her connection to him.

My gaze moves over the man currently grumbling into his phone about annoying little sisters and their inability to remember alarm codes.

"Thanks. I'll punch in the cancel code and reset the system." His hand lowers along with his head when he ends the call.

"Should we get dressed before going out there?" I ask.

His head snaps up, his eyes drilling into mine. "No. She gets us how she found us when she barged in at"—he checks his phone —"six-thirty am."

"Well, not quite how she found us." I smile. I can't tell if he's really pissed off or just trying to get his bearings after our rude awakening.

He barks a mirthless laugh. "True."

"I guess our day begins now." I look longingly at the bed we both just tumbled out of. "Do you have food or do you want me to order in breakfast?"

"I've got stuff here. I'll make omelets, you make coffee."

"You say that as if you think I'm capable."

"Of course, you are. You may have had everything brought to your suite yesterday, but I doubt that's what you do every day. You're not the type to let others wait on you."

I cock my head. "Think you've got me pegged?"

"Don't I?" he asks as he makes his way toward me.

"In this, yes."

He slips his arms around my waist and pulls me flush against him. "I might not know everything about you, Oakley, but I know enough."

"I think you might know more than most and that's a scary thought when we've only known each other two days."

"Why is that scary?"

"Well, once you know everything, you'll get bored and move on." I soften my words with a smile.

"I won't underestimate you, don't underestimate me."

"I'm not." I shake my head. "I was joking, Walker."

"Good. Because I will know every little thing about you and still want you."

I have to bite my tongue to stop the word 'promise' from slipping out.

He owes me no guarantees at this point in our relationship and we may have professed our love for each other last night but that isn't a guarantee either.

More than most, I know being loved by someone doesn't mean they'll stay with you.

"We need to talk about some of those things you don't know but I think we should deal with your sister first."

"How do you—" Shaking his head, he lets me go and spins me toward the bathroom. "Never mind. I'm sure your PI had that information for you. Go use the bathroom; I'll use the guest one and meet you in the kitchen."

I glance over my shoulder. "If you grab my bag from the foyer—"

"Nope. She gets us as is." He taps my ass lightly. "Now get going—the more I wake up, the hungrier I get. I need to replenish all the energy someone fucked out of me last night."

A shiver races over my skin. "Shit. Why'd you have to remind me? Now I'll be thinking dirty thoughts in front of your sister the first time I meet her."

"Like you weren't going to think them anyway," Walker says

with a cocky grin as he heads to his closet. "If you want some sweats, I've got a few draw-string pairs that might stay up."

"I thought she was getting us as is?"

"She was until you had me thinking about why I'm so hungry which gave me a boner."

My eyes drop to his groin. Oh, yeah, the briefs he pulled on aren't hiding a thing. Grinning, I head into the bathroom to pee and wash my face. I'm sure I've got last night's makeup all over it.

By the time I make it to the kitchen, Walker is busy at the stove and Shelby is sitting on a stool at the island, a mixing bowl in her lap, a whisk in her hand, beating the hell out of some eggs.

Neither of them sees me, which means I catch the tail end of their conversation.

"You didn't tell me you were seeing someone, and not just anyone for fuck's sake. Walker, you're screwing the CEO of Rogue!"

"Shel, I've never given you the details of my love life. Why would I start now?"

"Because before you were picking gold digging skanks!"

"Whoa." He lifts the frypan off the heat and turns to face his sister. "Is that what you really think?"

Shelby sighs and puts the bowl on the counter in front of her. "No. But none of them were anyone you would get serious about. This one is. And she doesn't live here. And you've got so many things happening..."

"You think this is a distraction from my life, is that what you're getting at?" He moves to stand on the opposite side of the island from her and reaches for her hands. When she places hers in his, he continues, "She's it for me."

"How long have you been seeing her? You haven't mentioned her once and now you're all over the internet with her on your arm."

"We've known each other for months, Shel, since before my injuries—"

"If she's the one, why wasn't she here?!"

"Ah, right. You think she's using me because she wasn't holding my hand during the last few months."

"What else would I think?"

"We've been taking things slow, and neither of us wanted to add the pressure of the world to our budding relationship."

I want to interrupt. I want to remind the woman of the relationship she's having behind closed doors. But I can't out her involvement with Walker's best friend any more than I can out the real reason her brother is retiring.

It's not my place.

"Promise me you'll be careful. I'm worried about this new shift in your professional life as it is."

"I can promise that. I'll also promise that I'm okay with the change to my career. Am I disappointed? Yes. Would I change it if I could? Hell, yes. Am I unhappy with the new path I'm taking? Fuck no. I can't explain it, but this new direction feels right. Feels more right than anything I've ever done and that rightness includes my relationship with Oakley."

"How'd you even meet her?"

"I'm the face of the new line of Rogue's sportswear for elite athletes."

"The photo shoot the other day? You've known her two days!"

"No. We met when I signed the sponsor deal last year, before my injuries."

"Oh. Okay. That's better than two days."

I can't help but cringe at the relief in her voice. If she knew the truth, and I have to admit I'm surprised he didn't tell her the real story, she would definitely be against us.

Maybe that's why Walker hasn't told her.

If we're going to pull this off, then the fewer people who know the real story, the better. It would only take one slip of the tongue for the press to eat it up, and neither of us needs that kind of attention right now.

Me more than him.

Not that I would let anything the media said affect the choices I make for either Rogue sportswear or the Rogues franchise.

"Now, when she comes out here, be nice," he instructs before getting back to the stove. "Have you finished with those eggs? The veggies are ready."

"Yeah." Shelby hops off the stool and walks around the island to deliver the egg mixture to her brother. "I'm sorry. It's just after you left yesterday, all I could think about was how your life has done a one-eighty and you can't play hockey anymore."

"Pour those in. I can keep playing, just not at a professional level."

"Same, same."

Walker laughs. "No. It's not. And I'll still be in the hockey world."

"You said that, but as what? You've never talked about anything but playing for as long as I've been alive."

"Trust me. This is good. And as soon as I can tell you, I will."

Shelby eyes her brother and I hold my breath waiting for her next words.

"Fine. But she better not screw you over. I don't care how rich she is, I'll take her down."

"As much as I love your defense of me, I don't need you to fight my battles, Shelby."

"You might not need me to but I'm going to. It's what little sisters are for."

"Ha! Little sisters are for pains in the ass."

"Hey! I've never been a pain in your ass." The arms she has crossed over her chest slowly lower. "Have I?"

"Ah, fuck. No." Walker wraps an arm around her neck and tugs her in for a hug. "Not once."

"I'm sorry I barged in here. I didn't even think about you not being alone..."

"It's okay. You get to meet Oakley sooner than I thought, but that's not a bad thing. You're going to love her."

"I googled her."

He let her go and put up his hand. "I don't want to know. You can't believe half the shit you read on the internet."

"She's worth billions! And she's older than you!"

"You say that like you think she's ancient."

"No, but she's thirty-two."

"And I'm turning twenty-nine next month."

"Actually, I'm thirty-three in a week," I say as I move into the room.

Shelby's face turns red and Walker grins. "Hey, come meet my sister. Properly this time."

"Is it really proper when I'm only wearing your shirt?" I ask with a grin. "Hello, Shelby, it's a pleasure to finally meet you. Your brother has told me so much, I feel as though we know each other already."

"Ah, hi, um…Oakley."

"Are you staying for breakfast? Want coffee?"

"Yeah," she glances at her brother. "Coffee would be great. I can get it."

"Nonsense. Take a seat, you're the guest; we'll take care of breakfast."

I need her to understand that I'm not a bystander to Walker's life. I'm part of it and that means preparing meals for anyone who visits our place.

Not that I'm assuming his place is mine…okay, maybe I am. After this morning's declarations of love, I think I'm allowed a little assumption.

"Walker said he modeled Rogue's new line the other day."

"Yes. It's for our elite line. The launch is next month."

What I don't say is I'm hoping it will take some of the focus off the franchise announcement but I'm thinking it.

"Let me get the coffee on and I'll grab my laptop and show you the proofs of the shoot."

"You've got those already?" Walker asks.

"Yep. Although I think we need to retake some of the ones in the longs. They're a little risqué."

He cocks an eyebrow.

"Nobody needs to know how many veins are on your dick, Walker."

"Eeewwww......" Shelby waves her hands in front of her. "Stop, stop, don't talk about my brother's junk. Jesus. I don't need that in my head."

Laughing, I glance between them. They're both red in the face and their discomfort only makes me laugh harder.

"It's not funny." He steps toward me and hooks his arm around my neck like he did with his sister. The only difference is the words he whispers in my ear. "I'm going to spank your ass later for that."

My whole body jolts, every muscle locking tight. I'm not sure what to call the sound that gurgles in my throat. It's a moan, a purr, a whimper, all rolled into a noise I can't hold inside.

"Huh. You're not opposed to that idea. Good to know."

"Walker." My voice has a quiet, husky edge.

"Um, should I leave..."

Walker turns us to face his sister and now I'm the one with a red face. But I don't back down from difficult situations and I keep my eyes on her.

"Wow. Okay." Her eyes land on her brother and soften. "I get it. It's palpable, like I can reach over and touch it."

The moment hangs. Shelby's words seem to echo around us or maybe they're just in my head.

I get what she's saying because I feel it. Whenever Walker is near there's a charge in the air. And the way he looks at me?

God. There's something visceral about the way he looks at me. A physical aspect to that blue-gray gaze that trails over me like fingertips leaving my skin coated in goose bumps.

I've never encountered it before. Don't know how to deal with it other than wrapping myself around him and kissing him stupid.

Except I can't do that every time he looks my way. Case in

point, last night. All the glances, the innocent touches, his warmth beside me.

I tilt my head so I can see his eyes. The emotions swirling in them steal my breath.

I may have said the words I love you and felt them before now but right here, in this moment in front of his sister, I know it doesn't matter what comes at us. We're going to make it.

I've never been more sure of anything in my life, and I was pretty damn sure about Rogue sportswear and the Rogues franchise. Hell, I put millions of dollars into both.

I'd put everything I have into Walker.

I'd lay it all on the line for us.

"Oak." His forehead lowers and rests on mine. "I..."

His eyelids lower over the storm gray clouds in his eyes and I know he's feeling this moment as deeply as I am.

It's scary how in sync we are. And yet it's not.

The rightness I feel being in his arms whether in or out of bed is a sensation I've never had before.

Not when we broke our first million in profit, not when I inked my name on a contract KAW had spent months vying for.

"Okay, you know what, I think I should leave."

"No!"

"Don't go."

We talk over each other as we whip around to look at Shelby but it's me who convinces her to stay.

"Please. I want to show you those proofs and I'd like to spend some time together. I feel like I know you through Walker but it's not the same as talking to you."

"I don't—" She huffs out a breath. "You know what, I'd like that too. I'll be honest, I was skeptical at first and I thought the pictures of the two of you online were staged but seeing you together this morning...yeah, if you don't mind me interrupting your day, I'd love to hang out a while."

"Excellent."

"Go get your laptop," Walker nudges me toward the living

room. "I'll get breakfast on the table, including coffee, in about ten minutes."

"You don't—"

"I really like the idea of you and my sister hanging out."

"Well, that's a first. Quick, Oakley, let's go before he changes his mind."

Shelby scoots around the kitchen island and hooks her arm through mine. I let her lead me away, but my gaze is on Walker.

I see love and pleasure in his gaze, and I have to wonder about Shelby's comment of this being a first. I don't wonder long.

"He's never let me hang out with any of his girlfriends. Not even that Krissy bitch," she mutters.

"Oh, you didn't like Kristina?"

A shudder wracks her. "Hell no. That's one obvious gold-digging skank I will be forever grateful he didn't introduce me to."

"Hmm...I struggle to understand how they stayed together so long."

"Oh, I wouldn't call what they had being together."

"You wouldn't?"

"Hell no. He'd go over there and screw her, then leave. I'm not sure they ever spent the whole night together."

"Really?" That bit of info hadn't been in the PI report. Then again, Walker had already broken things off with Kristina before I initiated the investigation.

"I don't think he's ever spent the night with a woman." Shelby hums as she thinks. "I'll have to ask Gannon to be sure, but I know in college he was a one and done guy."

The more she speaks, the more I like. Because he's stayed with me all night.

Twice.

WALKER

The media frenzy starts before my retirement announcement even leaves my agent's office.

Mine and Oakley's phones have been going crazy for the last hour. We've ignored them until now.

But as we usher Shelby out the door onto the street, the doorman helping her into the car Oakley ordered, I can see the paparazzi lining the sidewalk to the left and right as well as across the road.

"We're going to need to deal with them," Oakley murmurs. "It isn't fair to everyone else who lives in the building."

"I'll get the doorman to call the police. See if they can move them off."

"It might be better if we do a press conference." She glances up at me. "Has your agent sent your press release out yet?"

"I don't think so." I rub a hand on my chin, the stubble scratchy. "Let me call him and we can work out what to do."

"Let's conference call him to sort it out. I also think you should reach out to Rafe, ask him if they want to do a joint one."

"They said—" No, *they* didn't, Cantrell did, and after dinner last night I don't think I can take his word when it comes to the Knights org. "You're right. I should see what he wants to do."

Putting a hand on her lower back I urge her toward the elevator.

"I'll message Drake and let him know what's going on and see when he can—"

"Drake is right here."

We spin around to find Drake is indeed here. "Hey."

He's frowning at me. "You didn't think I should know about this?" He waves a hand between me and Oakley.

"Have I ever told you about my love life?"

"No, but you've never been seeing the billionaire CEO of a global sportswear company and if rumor has it"—he aims a look at Oakley that has my hackles rising—"the owner of a national sports team."

"What rumor," Oakley demands as I say, "Fuck!"

"Inside contacts. I do represent a number of hockey players, remember?" Drake puts his arm out. "Lead the way—the rest of this conversation needs to be out of the press's lens shot."

He's right, we can't hang around the building's foyer talking about this. "C'mon."

The quiet in the elevator is not a comfortable one. I can't come up with any words to ease it either. And a quick glance at Oakley shows me she's not going to make the effort.

Her mouth is set, her eyes focused, and I imagine the wheels in her head are spinning.

She's a talented businesswoman, there's no denying that, not with the success of Rogue and now the signing of a national sports franchise.

If anyone can navigate the turbulent waters to come, it's her. That's why I'll follow her lead. Professionally and personally.

I'm all in, after all.

I get the front door open and motion her and Drake in ahead of me.

Oakley is already striding toward the dining room. "I'll get my laptop set up for the call to..." She looks over her shoulder at Drake. "Nat and Blake," she finishes.

I know what she's doing. She's not about to confirm the rumor, at least not until she's spoken to her partners. She rarely mentions their fourth, Cami, because she's not part of the everyday decisions.

In fact, I think Cami is a journalist. Which may work in our favor if we can use her in any way to steer the media frenzy.

"Why the fuck didn't you tell me you were seeing Oakley James?" Drake hisses in my ear.

I give him a narrow-eyed look. "Careful with that tone."

His eyes widen and he takes a step back. "Wow. Okay. You've never used that look on me before. I've seen it, on the ice, in interviews, but never looked into it straight on."

He shakes his head and takes a step in the direction Oakley went. I don't bother saying anything because my teeth are still clenched tight on the anger that burst inside me at the sound of his voice.

"I'm going to make a quick call in the bedroom." Oakley walks toward me, phone in hand. "Can you put some coffee on?"

Her question is aimed at me but it's Drake who answers.

"I'll get it."

She arches an eyebrow and waits for him to be out of earshot before speaking. "Do you want in on the call?"

"To Nat and Blake? Why would I?"

"Because you might not have signed a contract, but you're part of the team now. A major part and I think as this is going to affect you, we should include you in the discussions and decisions on how to handle whatever the hell is about to blow up in our faces."

"No. I trust you to make the right decisions. Just let me know what they are." And I do trust her. Completely.

She smiles at me and pushes to her toes to lay a far too quick kiss on me. "Back in a bit."

She's gone before I can grab her and kiss her properly. The urge to follow is strong but I know we don't have time for that now. Besides, if I follow her into the bedroom, we're not coming out for a while.

A while we don't have.

Especially with my agent in my damn kitchen.

Sighing, I scrub a hand over my face and head in Drake's direction.

"Where'd you hear the rumor?" I ask without preamble.

"Cantrell."

"*Jerry?*" What the fuck?

"He was on the other end of my phone about thirty minutes ago. Told me he was suing the pants off us both because he knows you've signed to play with the new franchise that hasn't been announced yet."

If I thought my jaw was clenched before, I was an idiot. I'm clamping down so hard I swear I hear bones cracking.

"He said this thing between you and Oakley is a smoke screen to hide the deal."

"Huh." As theories go it's not a bad one. It's way off but it's not unbelievable.

"So is it a smoke screen?"

I laugh. "Did you not see me give you the look when you spoke about Oakley in a tone I didn't find acceptable?"

Drake puts his hands up. "Got it. Not a smoke screen."

Moving around him I get three mugs out of the cupboard. "I'm in love with her." I don't know why I feel the need to explain myself or give him the depth of our relationship but I do.

Hell, I want everyone in the world to know I'm in love with Oakley James.

"And she's…"

I give him another narrow-eyed look.

"Right. She's with you."

There's an awkward silence between us for a few moments and I don't feel the need to soothe it with words. I want him to feel uncomfortable about this discussion.

"Okay, so what do we do about your retirement announcement?"

"Nothing right this minute. We'll wait for Oakley to join us and I'll give Rafe a call—"

"Why are you calling Rafe?" Drake asks as he picks up the first mug to fill with coffee now the pot is full.

"Um…" I glance around, for who I haven't a clue because the only other person in the apartment is Oakley and she knows what I'm about to reveal. "This doesn't leave this apartment."

If Drake is taken aback by my tone, he doesn't show it. He pushes a mug across the counter toward me. "If this has to do with Jerry Cantrell getting a kick in the nuts, I'll keep my lips sealed, grab popcorn and a drink so I can sit back and watch the show."

"Good. He doesn't actually own the Knights."

"What? Who the hell does?"

"Laken Cantrell."

Drake's still for half a second then he cracks up laughing so hard he doubles over. He tries to speak but nothing forms that I can understand.

I get why he thinks it's hilarious. Before Gerald Senior died, his son was known as Gerald Junior. After Senior died, Junior made it clear he was no longer the junior in his family and everyone should call him Jerry.

"Oh fuck." Drake straightens and wipes at his eyes. "Please tell me I need that drink and popcorn."

"You will. I don't know the timeline, but I know Laken is making moves in the next week or so."

"Good time for you to cut ties with the Knights. Let's get that announcement out sooner than later," Drake says.

"Let me call Rafe real quick, then see what Oakley has to say."

"Why do we need Ms. James's input on this?"

"Because our relationship has been splashed all over the place this morning?" I don't mean for it to be a question but it comes out that way.

"And the rumor…" Drake raises an eyebrow. "You haven't confirmed or denied that."

"It's not Walker's job to confirm or deny." Oakley comes into the kitchen, her stride smooth, confident. "Care to tell me the details of the rumor?"

"Sure. Like I just told Walker, Jerry Cantrell called this morning to inform me he was suing me and him because he *knows* you've signed Walker to play on your new team."

The smile that tips her mouth is full of humor. "Any idea where he got that from?"

"No. I told him I had no idea what he was talking about and I don't speculate on my clients' relationships, to which he said the thing between you two is a smoke screen to cover up your back-stabbing ways."

She's laughing now and I have to chuckle along with her because Oakley doesn't need to backstab anyone to get what she wants.

"Walker tell you Jerry doesn't own the Knights?"

"He did indeed reveal that hilarious piece of info."

"Good." Turning to me she says, "I spoke to Nat and Blake and I have an NDA here." Her gaze flicks to Drake.

"Ah, sure. If that's the way you want it to go." I'm trying not to reveal too much. Drake's a smart man, he'll be putting everything together to form a big picture. Proving that thought correct, he speaks.

"Got a pen for me to sign that NDA?"

Oakley's mouth tips up on one side. "Oh, I think I like him."

"You better." He offers her a mug. "We're going to be doing business together in the future, I'm sure."

She takes the coffee and heads for the dining room. "C'mon, let's put a plan of action together so we can all get on with the real business of our day."

When she's out of earshot Drake moves closer to me and says with a grin, "I think I like her too."

"You better. I plan on keeping her around."

"I figured."

We follow Oakley and within a minute Drake has signed on the dotted line and we're sitting around the table, my phone in the middle on speaker, waiting for Rafe to answer.

"Walker," Rafe answers. "What can I do for you?"

"My announcement. Do the Knights want to make it a joint one?"

"Ah, give me a second."

We hear a lot of moving around and the distinct sound of a door closing.

"Okay, I want to say yes but the shit hit the fan here this morning. Laken is with the team lawyers now."

"Is she okay?" Oakley asks, shifting forward in her seat, concern etched on her face, in the stiffness of her posture.

"She will be."

"Does she need anything?"

"No. But thank you."

"Tell her to call me any time."

"I will. Now, Walker, have you spoken to your agent—"

"I'm here too."

"Right. Full court press. Okay, can you put the announcement off until later today or tomorrow?"

I glance at Oakley who shrugs, then Drake who gives me a thumbs up. "Yeah, we can hold off. What are you thinking?"

"Well, we're going to be defending the team and Laken against Cantrell but not yet. The lawyers have done their thing, and he now has a gag order on him that should prevent him from talking more. But it's Jer, so anything is possible."

I bite my tongue to keep from saying what I'm thinking but Oakley doesn't have the same restraint.

"He's an idiot. He's already spreading rumors about the league's new franchise, and you and I both know the league will not take kindly to him revealing any information on that deal before they do."

"Wow. His idiocy never stops." Rafe's sigh comes through

loud and clear. "Let's talk again tomorrow and set up a press conference for the day after, Walker."

"I'm good with that."

"Okay, talk then. I'm sorry to cut this short but I gotta get back to Laken."

"Go. And thanks. I'll wait to hear from you tomorrow."

"All right. Bye."

When the line goes dead, Drake leans back in his chair. "Well. That's one thing dealt with, what's next?"

"Now I have your pretty signature, I think we talk about this." Oakley drops a bundle of papers I recognize in front of him.

He barely reads the first paragraph before his eyes are up and he says, "It's true?"

"Yep." She nods with a Cheshire cat smile. "You're the first, outside of the league and KAW, to know the newest NHL team is the Rogues coming out of Baton Rouge."

"Holy shit." He tips sideways and pulls out his phone. "I need to make a call to someone."

I look at Oakley. "Shouldn't you notify the league of the leak?"

"No. Better if it comes from direct sources." She points to Drake, then pushes back her chair and stands. "C'mon, let's make sure we don't overhear anything. That way we can deny knowledge about this call without lying."

"I need a refill," I say as I stand.

Reaching for Drake's mug, I hook a finger through the handle. It's heavier than I thought, and he probably doesn't need a refill but it'll keep us out of the room long enough for him to make the call.

She waits until we're in the kitchen before speaking, her voice lowered. "Are you going to reveal I offered you a job?"

"I don't know. Should I?"

"Up to you. I've just told him about the Rogues so it's not like you have to be vague."

"True. And I did wonder if I needed an agent for the contract."

"Get him and your lawyer to look at it but unless you have completely unrealistic demands, we're open to modifying the contract to fit your needs."

"Is that because we're sleeping together or because you want me to coach the team?"

"I'd never give you special consideration because we're having sex, and it's more than that anyway."

"It is." I nod and lean my hip against the counter while she tops up all the mugs. "How much more?"

"Huh?" She glances at me. "What do you mean?"

"How much more do we want to make this now? We're obviously not hiding our relationship anymore, and I'm about to announce my retirement..." Rubbing a hand over my jaw, I make a mental note to shave. "Should we establish the seriousness of us for the world to see to defuse some of the gossip that's bound to circulate once the Rogues are announced?"

"How? Us being seen together, you moving in with me isn't enough?"

"Well..." The more I think about it, the more I'm convinced my line of thought is a good one. "Got time for a quick holiday?"

She's got her mug halfway to her mouth but stops. Putting it down, she doesn't take her eyes off me. "You are not thinking what I think, are you?"

I grin. "Depends what you're thinking I'm thinking."

"Walker." My name is a warning, but I see the spark of excitement in her eyes. I know she's not totally averse to what I'm suggesting.

And I'm not even being clear.

"We can't," she adds when I push off the counter.

"Sure, we can."

"Walker." She takes a step back.

I follow.

"Walker." She's trembling now and I reach for her hand, steady it in mine.

"Oak."

Her eyes close and I know I have her. When she looks at me again, a smile takes over my face and I lower to one knee.

She sucks in a breath and the fingers of the hand I hold—her left one—curl tightly around mine.

Then I say two words. And they're more demand than question.

"Marry me."

OAKLEY

I'm nodding.

Holy shit.

I'm nodding.

And grinning.

And shit, shit, shit.

I'm in his arms, my mouth on his, and we're tumbling to the floor.

His hands are under my shirt, mine under his, our mouths eating at each other in a desperate attempt to sate the crazy maelstrom of emotions engulfing us.

"Ah, should I leave?"

We rip apart. Pant like we've been starved of oxygen for a week, and stare at each other with grins so wide I'm sure we look like a couple of lunatics.

Hell, at this point I think we are lunatics.

As one we turn our heads to look up at Drake who's standing at the edge of the kitchen island with a look on his face I can't decipher. It could be fear.

That thought stretches my mouth wider. He steps back, gives us a quizzical look, and my grin turns into laughter.

"What am I seeing here?"

"You are seeing the happiest man on the planet," Walker says.

I open my mouth to speak, to say *and woman*, but I don't get a chance because one second I'm on the floor wrapped around him and the next I'm on my feet with Walker's arms around me from behind, his chin resting on my shoulder.

"She just agreed to marry me."

He sounds so happy. Like I've given him the thing he wants most in the world, and I'd be lying if I said I don't feel the joy of what we just decided.

"She what? Jesus Christ, you two are certifiable." Drake shakes his head. "You know this is crazy, right?"

"Maybe it would be for you, but it doesn't feel crazy to me, it feels right. Like this is what I'm supposed to be doing." Walker tightens his arms around me. "Like I'm right where I'm meant to be."

I absorb his words and lean into him harder. They're both right. This is crazy but it does feel right.

I've always followed my gut. Yes, I'm smart and I use my intellect too, but sometimes that takes a backseat, and every time in my life that it has, that I've jumped in feet first, I've come out a winner.

Rogue sportswear, going after a national hockey franchise, both faced opposition when we started the process of getting them off the ground. And while the second hasn't proven itself yet, it will. I know it will.

Walker and I feel the same.

It's the same bone-deep knowledge that this is right. We're both exactly where we should be.

Hell, I didn't even think about it before I was nodding. That says everything.

Shaking his head, Drake reaches for his mug. "All right, let's get a plan of some sort together before you lovebirds fly away."

"How do you know we're flying somewhere?" Walker asks.

"I'm sensing things move at warp speed with you two, so it makes sense that you'd fly to Vegas and do the deed. The question is are you going before or after we deal with the clusterfuck Cantrell has stirred up. Oh, and Oakley, expect a phone call from the league sometime today."

"Shit." I untangle myself from Walker. "I don't need this crap. I wish I could punch Jerry in the face."

"Get in line," Drake calls over his shoulder as he heads back to the dining room.

"As much as I want to join in with you bloodthirsty people, I'm going to sit back and watch Laken take a shredder to him."

I grin. "Oh yeah, and don't forget Rafe. I get the feeling that man will pulverize anything left over."

"Hey, maybe you should give Laken or Rafe a heads up. I think the league is unaware of the fact Jerry does not own the Knights. They were talking about fines for him leaking the information to me," Drake says when we join him.

"How'd he get the info?"

"No idea."

I ponder that and the only conclusion I can come to is someone inside the league gave it to him.

"I think the league has a leak. No one outside the KAW board, and that's only four of us, and you two know about the contract I signed two days ago."

"KAW as in Rogue sportswear's parent company?" Drake asks.

"Yes."

"Right. So someone inside told Cantrell and he told me..."

"Who the hell would reveal it to Cantrell?" Walker asks. "Nobody likes him that much do they?"

"No, they don't and—"

It hits me. Like a slap upside the head the knowledge slams into my brain. I know exactly who got the information and passed it on to Jerry.

"Fuck! Motherfucking slut!"

"Whoa, whoa, whoa, where are you going?" Walker tries to hold me in place.

"To open a file. I need to double check my memory is correct before I go all guns blazing after that bitch."

He lets go of my hand and I race over to my laptop. I already have my phone out, dialing Nat before I even hit a key.

"Hey, I didn't—"

"Shut up and listen. The info Jerry told Drake I mentioned earlier came from Dugan."

"Dugan? How do you know that?" Nat asks.

"Because he's in bed with Kristina."

"Well fuck." Nat sighs. "I knew I should have come with you to New York."

"Get on the first plane you can. If it's not soon enough, I'll send the jet. No wait. Call Pa. Get him to fire up the family one."

"I'm not using your grandfather's plane!"

"I need it anyway. Don't worry. I'll call him next. Just get to the airport."

"Oakley—"

"Do it, Nat. And bring Blake. I think we're moving the announcement forward. It's the only way to get on top of this."

"Fuck, fuck, fuck. We don't need this bullshit. We'll have enough to deal with when the old boys find out we got the team."

"One battle at a time. Get Blake and get up here."

"See you in a few hours. And keep me posted on what you're organizing."

"Will do." I don't bother saying goodbye. I've got too much to pull together and Nat knows it.

Once I open up the file I'm looking for, I skim through the report and find the dates I need. I'm noting them, as well as scribbling down possible ways to deal with this as they occur to me and hoping this doesn't blow up our dreams.

"I hope to fuck those bastards don't break our contract," I mutter.

"Get in front of it and they won't. They can't anyway. The backlash would be horrendous if they pulled it for something you didn't do. It would look like they freaked out about your gender. Or we could make it look that way."

My gaze snaps to Drake's and a slow smile curls my mouth. "Oh, I really do like you."

"What do you need me to do?" Walker asks.

"Call Rafe. Let him know what's going on with Jerry. You can tell him Drake gave you the info; you don't have to reveal who he said got the team. Just give him the bare bones so he knows the league is going to want to punish the Knights."

"They can't penalize them when he's not the owner, can they?"

"Probably not but they'd need to know that," Drake adds.

"I think this scandal may eclipse the franchise announcement."

I glance at Walker. "Let's hope so. Although if it does, it won't distract them for long."

"We don't need them distracted forever. Just long enough to get some things put in place."

Drake clears his throat. "And by your use of *we* I'm assuming you're looking to be involved with the new team?"

"Ah…"

I hide a grin. Walker just put his foot in it if his plan was to keep Drake in the dark about his new job. His sigh filled with resignation makes me laugh.

"Yeah, I'm involved. Oakley?"

"Up to you." I'm still reading and something that I should have noticed before jumps out at me. "Well, shit."

"What now?"

"She's also been in bed with Lilibeth Mortimer."

"The wife of Boris Mortimer?"

"Yep."

"Jesus."

"I'm so glad your taste in women has improved in recent years, Walker." Drake has a point.

I don't bother to hide my grin this time. "Me too."

"Getting back to what we were talking about." Drake says. "How big is your involvement?"

"They've offered me head coach."

When the silence drags on a bit I look up. What I find is Drake struck dumb. His mouth opens and closes and honestly, the confusion on his face is a little annoying.

"What? You don't think he's a good choice?"

"I, no... but..." He shakes his head; hopefully it clears it so he can remember all that Walker has achieved. "You want him to coach the newest hockey team in the league?"

"Yes. We do." I stand up straight, hold up a hand. "And before you give me the same bullshit excuses Walker did to try to convince me our choice is wrong, let me say this. Take a few minutes to think about his career on and off the ice. Only then will I let *you* try to convince me. Not that you can."

"Huh." Drake folds his arms over his chest and leans back in the chair.

A quick glance at Walker shows he's grinning at me. He mouths *thank you* and I get back to pulling information together from the PI's file.

A few minutes later Drake interrupts me.

"Where's his contract?"

I can't stop the smirk. "Walker? In my briefcase in the bedroom."

I don't need Drake to say anything else. He's said it all by asking for the contract. But when Walker leaves the room, he speaks anyway.

"He'll be the youngest coach in the league."

"I know."

"He'll also be a fucking good one."

"He will. But he'll be more."

Drake chuckles. "Damn if you didn't snag a better option than any other coach out there I can think of."

"His assistant coach is Blake Watts."

"Well, fuck me. You've got the big guns—wait. Isn't she part of Rogue sportswear?"

"Yes, she's one quarter of KAW."

"If I remember right, KAW is four women."

"It is." I raise my gaze to watch his face.

"Damn. Any chance you need an in-house agent?"

Laughing I lower my eyes back to my notepad. "You'll be my first call if we do."

"Always wanted to live somewhere warm," is Drake's reply.

Grinning, I keep my head down and get back to lining up all the information I have on Kristina Bancroft's many and varied rendezvous with several people either in or connected to the NHL.

"Here. Should I read it before you?" Walker places his contract in front of Drake.

"You can't sign it yet and I've never steered you wrong on a contract before."

"True. True." Walker pulls out a chair but before he sits, asks, "Anyone need a top up, some food? Should I order in something for lunch?"

I note the time and consider how full I am from our breakfast with Shelby. "I'm good for food but maybe put another pot of coffee on in about ten minutes."

"I'll pass on the coffee, but I'll take a glass of cold water," Drake murmurs distractedly.

Walker leaves to fulfill Drake's request and I finish logging dates and names from the PI's report on Kristina when my phone rings.

I stare at the device as it vibrates on the table.

"You should answer it."

I look at Drake. "I'm not sure I'm ready yet. I need to get a few things straight in my head first."

"Okay, let it go to voicemail then..." He trails off as it does exactly that.

"I don't want them in charge of the announcement. Or at least I don't want them doing it without KAW there."

"So don't let them. Ask for a joint press conference. Make it seem as though you're deferring to them but nudge them in the direction you want to go. Do you have anything ready to go?"

"We do. And I may have a way to get the league to agree with my timeline too."

"Oh?"

"Cami, KAW's fourth. Her father owns the FNB Network. I can get access to their New York station. Hijack the seven o'clock sports news maybe."

"Do it. If you can give them a time and a place before they even suggest doing a press conference or release, you'll be in control."

Grinning at Drake, I say, "I really do like you."

"Hey, I was being serious about the job."

"I might just take you up on it."

Walker comes back with iced water for all of us. "Called Rafe. Told him shit was going down with the league and Cantrell was in the middle of it. Didn't tell him what, just said Cantrell had leaked some info he shouldn't have to Drake, who called a league contact."

He flops into a chair and leans back, arm crossed over his chest. The position shouldn't get me going but there's no denying the simmer of lust popping in my veins.

"We're getting married." It's not a question. I know the words are true and saying them out loud makes them more so. Not to mention the smile it puts on my face.

"Damn straight, we are." He unfolds his arms and leans toward me. "As soon as we fix this cluster, we'll get to work organizing the wedding. Do you want a big one?"

"No. I like Drake's idea."

"Vegas?"

"Maybe. I need to call Pa." Shit. I forgot about getting the jet ready for Nat and Blake.

Scooping up my phone, I hit speed dial one, speaker and put the device on the table beside my laptop.

Pa answers on the second ring. "What have you done now?"

"Huh? I've done nothing... Shit. Did someone call you?"

"Yeah, that suck-up Dugan."

"Dugan called you? He's the one who leaked the info!"

"Did he now? Well, that changes a few things. I'll call the pilot, be there in a few hours."

"Can you bring Nat and Blake with you?"

"Of course. You girls should have been together for this to begin with. I told you that."

"It wouldn't have stopped this from happening."

"Probably not, but you wouldn't be dealing with it on your own either."

"I'm not. As soon as I hang up, I'm calling Cami. I need to highjack FNB's New York studios."

"I'll get the other two to you, I'm assuming Cami isn't going to want to come."

"Ha! She wants nothing to do with it other than vague details *after* things happen."

"She'll come around."

"She hasn't with Rogue."

"No, but from what Fenton tells me, she's getting mighty frustrated with her job lately."

"Oh, why? She hasn't said anything to us."

"Fenton didn't go into the details other than he's hoping she'll break away from the paper and do her own thing."

"I want her on our media team, but she's being stubborn."

"Sounds like someone I know." I can hear the smile in Pa's voice. "Anyway, call if you need anything else; I'll round the girls up and see you soon."

Pa hangs up before I can thank him or say goodbye and when I look up, the two men are staring at me. "What?"

"Fenton Barnes? Your Pa knows Fenton Barnes?" Drake asks.

"Yeah, him, Fenton and Gerald are—were—best friends. My Grams used to call them the triple threat."

"Wait. Wait." Walker holds up his hands. "You grew up with Cantrell?"

I shake my head. "No. He's older than me."

"Not by much."

"Enough. Plus Pa never wanted me around him. I hung out with them whenever they got together. Gerald is the one who told us to go for the franchise."

"Gerald Cantrell Senior told you to bid for a NHL team?" Drake asks with a shake of his head.

"He did. But we were already talking about it because of Blake."

"Why because of her? She played professionally—why would she want to own a team?" Walker asks.

"Because we all saw what those women go through to get to that level, the shit that goes on behind closed doors."

"Then why not a women's team?"

"We'll go after one of those next."

Drake laughs. "You wanted to start with the hard shit first, then move to the easier."

"And that right there is why we went after the men's league. Since when is the women's league easier? Why do you even think that?"

"Huh." Drake sits back. "Damn. I didn't even realize what saying that implies."

"We know physically there are differences between men and women but the game is the same. Plus," I add with a grin. "There's nothing more satisfying than proving women are just as capable as men in an area traditionally controlled by men."

Drake grins. "It's going to be like watching a cat among the pigeons."

"Oh?"

"Yeah, you ladies are going to go in there and slaughter them all."

WALKER

"Do you want me in there with you? Or will I wait out here?" I give her the option because I want to support her the best way I can. And if that means I stay out of sight, then I stay out of sight.

"I think we should get people used to seeing us together. We've already been splashed all over the internet today, this isn't going to make anything worse."

"It won't make it better either."

She slips her arms around my waist and looks up at me. "I don't want you to hide. Don't want us to hide. I'm not planning to keep our relationship a secret so I don't see why you should wait out here when you can be in there."

Wrapping my arms around her, I pull her closer. "I don't want to hijack your conference."

"How?"

"By drawing attention away from you. From the Rogues announcement."

"I don't care if you do." She shrugs. "It might make it easier to avoid certain questions if you're there to distract the press."

"You're not going to announce anyone other than KAW owning the team and where they'll be located, right?"

"Right. When we announce other things, I want it to be

about the Rogues and nothing else. Right now it's us, the leaked info, and the league." She shakes her head. "Not to mention Cantrell's part in it. *I* don't mind sharing the spotlight but when I'm discussing team details, I want nothing taking away from that."

"Okay. I'll be by the door." I press a finger to her lips before she can speak. "I won't hide but I'm just the supportive partner today. Next time I'll be up there with you."

She grins against my finger. "I want us to have matching jewelry by then."

My mouth curls up in a smug smirk because I already know the ones I want. "Oh, we'll definitely have those by then."

"We're ready." Natalie Redding, the Rogues GM, marches toward us. "Dugan is making the announcement about the franchise, and he'll make it short and to the point."

"Did you give him the words we prepared?" Oakley turns in my arms so she can face Natalie.

"Yes. I explained our stance on the situation and that we'll gladly see them in a court of law or public opinion if he doesn't do this our way. He knows he fucked up. Knows the fact the franchise was linked to you in the media is on their heads, not ours."

"Good. I don't want enemies before we start but we can't just roll over and play dead when they fuck up either. They need to be held accountable. We held up our end of the deal."

Natalie nods. "Agreed."

"Is Cami pissed?"

I haven't seen Cami or Blake yet but they're both here somewhere. According to Oakley, her Pa decided even if Cami doesn't want anything to do with the day-to-day running of the team, as a partner of KAW she should be present for this conference.

I'd love to have been a fly on the wall to see how he got the woman on a plane to New York on such short notice.

"She was. Blake talked her down. And she's promised to be in on all the decisions even though she says she won't have any input."

Oakley laughs. "So she'll just be in the room or on the call when things come up?"

Natalie sighs. "Look, I know you think we should all be involved but I think she's right in staying out of it. She has no interest in the sport, no real knowledge of the game or how to run a professional team, *but* she did get this organized for us on short notice so it's not like she's putting nothing in."

Oakley holds up a hand. "I know. I get it, I just thought..." She shakes her head. "Never mind. It's not like she's had much input on Rogue sportswear over the years."

"We don't need her to put in on this either. We've all got our roles, and the ones we don't fill, we will hand over to capable experts."

I choke and cover it with a fist to my mouth and a fake cough.

"Something to say, Mr. Alcott?" Natalie asks me, her eyes narrowed, assessing.

"Ah." Fuck, that look makes me want to cup my balls. I clear my throat. "I'm not sure expert is the right word for me."

"Of course, it is. Don't sell yourself short or be short sighted." She leans closer. "If you think for one second I would put someone in a position they weren't capable of doing, you'd be an idiot and you're not."

"I." No more words form so I snap my mouth shut.

She indicates the direction she came from. "Now, let's get your girlfriend in there and get this thing over and done."

Spinning on her spiked heel, she stalks off, and I'm not sure how I feel about the woman.

I know she's one of Oakley's closest friends, her business partner, and they've known each other for years, but she's brash and I think maybe a little mean.

"Her bark is worse than her bite. In fact, she barks so she doesn't have to bite. Plus there's the whole dickhead husband thing she's got going on."

"Husband?"

The sigh she emits is heartfelt. "Yeah. I'll tell you about it later."

"I'm not sure if I'm looking forward to that conversation or not."

"Not. Johnathon—not John—Whitman is not a man you want to know."

"You don't like him, and she married him?"

"They were married before we met. At this point I'm pretty sure it's in name only. Oh, and her checking account. He hasn't had a real job in years and I'm not even sure what he's qualified to do anyway. As far as I know, she hasn't even told him about the Rogues franchise."

"How can she be married to him and not tell him?"

Oakley shrugs. "I don't know if they even talk, and she never takes work home or leaves anything like her phone where he can see it."

"Wow. I think you're right. I'm not looking forward to hearing about or meeting this guy."

"You'll have to at some point, I guess."

"And I guess we should stop talking and get in there before she comes back and barks at us again."

Laughing, she links her arm through mine, and says, "Let's go and get this done."

When we enter the room, I'm surprised how orderly everyone is. I don't know why I expected chaos, but I figured there would at least be some shouting going on.

Moving to the side of the door, I lean against the wall while Oakley talks with Natalie, Blake, who I know vaguely through her hockey career and her brothers, and a woman I'm assuming is Cami.

They have their heads together whispering and I glance over to see Rodney Dugan and Boris Mortimer frowning at them.

My spine stiffens and I'm on the verge of moving over to the men when Oakley looks in my direction. Sending me a wink, she smiles and turns. With her shoulders back and head up, she moves toward the two men.

They speak for a few seconds then all four women follow them to the microphone perched on a podium. It kind of reminds me of a White House press conferences and I smile when I think of Oakley in that place.

She'd raise hell, kick ass, and take names if she ever decided to go into politics.

"Evening, everyone. Thanks for joining us on short notice," Dugan says into the microphone. "We'll keep things short and sweet so you can all get home to your families and dinner plans."

"Is there—"

Dugan holds up a hand. "Please, we've prepared a statement. If you can keep your questions until later. Thanks."

Taking a breath, the man tugs at the cuffs of his shirt, and from here I can see the sweat beading on his forehead.

"We had planned this to be a little more celebratory but as information has found its way out to the public, we'll have to go without what we had in mind."

He glances at the four women behind him, his smile apologetic.

Facing front again he leans closer to the mic and says, "It's with great pleasure that we announce the winning bid for the National Hockey League's expansion franchise. KAW, the parent company of the globally successful Rogue sportswear brand, is the proud owner of the league's newest hockey team."

He takes a breath while numerous reporters yell out questions. Ignoring all of them, he continues with what I'm assuming is the speech Natalie gave him.

"We're excited to expand our reach south, and I'll step aside and let KAW CEO, Oakley James, give you the details of the new team."

Stepping forward, Oakley moves into Dugan's position. "Thank you, Rodney."

I can't help smiling at the use of his first name. Most of the owners and GMs call the league executives by their first names and I'm thrilled she's not shying away from doing it just because she doesn't have a penis.

"As Rodney said, two days ago, KAW was awarded the league's expansion franchise. It won't come as a surprise when I tell you the new team will be the Rogues, but you might not feel the same when I say the team will be based in Baton Rouge in a seven hundred million dollar arena and training facility."

The questions drown out anything else she says and there are a few reporters on their feet now. I have to admire her as she patiently waits out the furor.

Once the noise dies down, she looks around the room before speaking again.

"We're thrilled and excited and looking forward to joining the central division the season after next."

"Who's the coach?" someone shouts from the back of the room.

"We're not announcing staffing or players at this time. We'll be sure to let you know when we are."

"When will the arena be ready?" someone else calls out.

"We will be making more announcements in the coming weeks. Until then you can direct any inquiries to the Rogues website."

Shit. We've got a website? I'm pulling my phone from my pocket to look it up when some yells her name.

Glancing up I see everyone heading my way. Looks like the conference is over.

"Oakley!" Her name is shouted again. "You owe us answers!"

I can't see who called out the demand disguised as a question, but I know the second she decides to respond to it.

She stops, frozen in place for a second while everyone else continues toward me.

Turning slowly on her heel, Oakley leaves everyone behind and moves back in front of the mic.

Standing tall, her gaze scans the room before stopping near

the back on someone I can't see. "I owe you answers?" she asks, her voice portraying confusion when I know she's anything but.

"You're being tight-lipped about your plans—"

"Let me educate you on a few things. One, *I* owe you nothing. Two, any plans *I* have or do not have are irrelevant. Three, the question you should be asking is what does the Rogues organization have planned. And four, because I'm in a great mood and feeling generous, the Rogues plan to build a winning hockey team, a family, a community, that everyone involved with, including the fans, is proud of. Anyone outside of that doesn't matter."

"That attitude won't win you friends in the league."

Oakley laughs, the sound echoing through the room. "We're not here to win friends. We're here to win hockey games."

Multiple questions fly at the podium, but Oakley ignores them and once again turns to face me. She doesn't need to speak for me to know the conference is now officially over. And like the dedicated partner I am, I follow my woman out of the room.

I hear my name called out and it's the first time anyone has acknowledged my presence. Ignoring the shouting behind me, I close the door and follow the others into a room across the hall.

When I close that door, Oakley and Natalie are talking with Dugan and Mortimer and I can see neither man is happy.

If they think they're going to blame the mess we left in the other room on these women, they're in for a rude awakening.

None of these women are about to back down. If they were men, and this debacle was happening, the league would be making a public apology.

I doubt that will happen.

Then again, these women seem capable of anything, so I won't be surprised if there is one in the coming weeks.

Or if not an apology, at least extra effort in helping the Rogues off the ground.

I can't help smiling, I can't imagine the women of KAW wanting anyone's help.

"Hey." I turn to find Blake standing beside me.

"Blake." I hold out a hand. "Great to see you."

"Same." We shake, then she leans closer and lowers her voice. "Any chance we can convene at your place for some private conversation?"

"Of course. There's room for you all to stay."

"Oh, I think the plan is to head out tonight but thank you."

"Back to Baton Rouge?"

"No. We've got a plan to get you two hitched then we're hunting a hot shot."

She's grinning and I have no idea at what, but it's contagious and I smile back at her. "Are you talking a firefighter..."

"Nope. Although I have heard his slap shot referred to as being on fire."

"A player?"

"I find it funny how you didn't blink when I mentioned getting you two hitched."

"That wasn't the surprising part of your statement."

"Guess not." She tips her chin up. "They're heading out."

We watch in silence as Dugan and Mortimer leave. No one says a word for a good minute before Natalie turns to face me.

"The car's out front to take us to your place."

I glance at Oakley. "Let's go then."

"We're waiting until the security team gives us the all-clear."

"Security team?"

"They came in with these three." She indicates her partners. "Pa insisted."

"Okay. Are they coming with us to my place too?"

She nods. "They will. They'll station themselves around the entrances to your building until we're ready to go."

"I heard we're getting hitched then going hunting for a hot shot."

Oakley looks at Blake. "You found him?"

"No. But my brothers are working on it and I think this guy"

—she thumbs in my direction—"might have a few ideas of where to look too."

"If you give me a name…"

"Not here." Oakley's phone beeps and she looks at the screen. "Let's go."

Opening the door for the women, I see a couple of men in dark suits waiting. They couldn't look any more security if they had the word tattooed on their foreheads.

If we're going for discreet, we've failed before we get out of the building. If we're going for masculine power and stay-back vibes, we've got that shit down.

But then I think about the women I'm with and the amount of money they're worth.

I'm surrounded by billions in human form.

The enormity of their wealth hits me.

I'm no chump when it comes to money, but these four women have me beat hands down.

Some men might be intimidated by the success surrounding me. Me? I love it.

I know they were all born with wealth, but each of them has shown their worth by founding a globally successful brand worth billions in its own right.

Yeah, intimidated isn't what I'm feeling.

It's awe.

They could have used their trust funds to live a cushy life. Instead, they used a small amount each to build an empire.

I wouldn't be surprised if Rogue sportswear is worth more than their trust funds combined.

"Hey, what are you thinking about?"

"How in awe I am of you four."

"Really?"

"Yes. And back there you proved why you're so successful."

She arches an eyebrow at me.

"You didn't flinch when the shit hit the fan. You just got

down to work to clean it up and you did it in a way that left no one looking like an idiot."

"I'm pretty sure they felt like idiots."

"Well, yeah, but that's because you revealed the mistress of one is sleeping with the wife of the other. As well as Cantrell."

"They were not happy when I gave them that information."

"I'm expecting to hear from her about this."

"I've got things in place to stop that. I've also got Shelby covered because I think Kristina might go there when she can't get to you."

"Shelby moved in with Gannon. He'll keep her safe."

Oakley hums. I can't decide if she agrees with me or not.

"You don't think he will?"

"Oh, I know he will, but I've got it covered as well to give you extra peace of mind."

Bending, I drop a kiss on her forehead. "Thank you for thinking of my sister while dealing with this mess."

"She's important to you so she's important to me."

Her words say it all.

And make me fall in love with her a little deeper.

OAKLEY

"Everything okay," Walker whispers in my ear.

"Yes. Why wouldn't it be?"

"You're being really quiet."

"I'm just enjoying this."

"This?"

"Yeah, you and my closest friends getting on like a house on fire."

And they are. Sure, there was the usual tension between Nat and any new person but once we got back to Walker's and she relaxed, that changed.

"What can I say? I'm a likable guy." He grins at me.

"Yes, you are. And you're my guy." Why I feel the need to reinforce that is beyond me except I like saying it so I don't fight the urge.

And I like *knowing* it.

"Speaking of that. I've got something to show you." He stands and offers me a hand.

"I've seen what you've got," I laugh but take his help and get to my feet.

"I'm not showing you that!" He's laughing too and it draws everyone's attention.

171

"Where are you two going? Do we need to leave?" Nat asks.

"No. We'll be back in a minute."

He doesn't explain further, just leads me from the room toward his bedroom.

"Are you sure we don't need to go?" Blake yells behind us.

"No!" Walker yells just as loud.

I can't help the grin that splits my face. I really do like how well they're all getting on. After the disaster that is Nat's husband, I had some concerns but I should have known not to worry.

Walker is real where Johnathon Whitman is anything but. Shaking my head, I clear it of any thoughts of Nat's husband. I don't want him ruining whatever it is Walker has in mind.

When we get to the bedroom, he moves me in front of the windows and says, "Wait here."

He disappears into his closet and I can hear him moving things around, a drawer opening and closing followed by another and then some muttered cursing.

"Everything all right in there?" I call out.

"Fine. Give me a minute."

There are more drawers opening and closing and then I hear 'aha!'.

He must have found what he was looking for because he comes striding out of the closet like the winner of the Cup being presented with his prize.

"I should have done this earlier, but I went with the right moment instead of the staged one." Dropping to a knee in front of me, he reaches for my left hand and looks up at me. "I know I asked already, I know you said yes, but I'm asking again."

I open my mouth to tell him he doesn't have to do this when what he has in his other hand grabs my attention. "*Oh*."

"These were my parents' rings. I'd be honored if you wore my mother's, if I wore my father's. Oakley James, will you give me the greatest gift in the world and let me be your husband?"

"My answer is still yes. And those are gorgeous. I'd be more than honored to wear them. But..." I drop to my knees in front of him. "Does Shelby know you're doing this? Is she okay with me having them?"

"I..." He snaps his mouth shut and closes his eyes. "Shit!"

"I don't want to ruin the moment, but I can't accept them until I know Shelby is okay with it."

Walker's eyes are blazing when they open. "This. This is why I fell for you in an instant."

Tilting my head to the side, I eye him.

"You have the biggest, most generous heart. I don't think you even realize you're thinking of everyone else all the time. You weigh everything up so quickly and know the best way to get what you want without hurting others."

"Oh." His words touch me deeply, so deeply my sight blurs and the sting of tears burns my nose. "Walker."

"Come here." He pulls me in, wraps his arms around me, and lets me rest my head on his chest.

"I don't know how you see me so well," I murmur.

"I don't either, but I do, and I want to see you for the rest of our lives."

"We will. But I'm serious about those rings. And I have an idea that may work for all of us."

"What is it?"

"What if we use the wedding bands and give Shelby the engagement and eternity rings?"

"She's never mentioned Mom's rings so I just assumed she didn't want them. Now I see that was foolish thinking. Of course, she'll want the option to have them. But if she doesn't, will you wear them?"

"Of course! And if she does take them, I'd like to have something similar made for us. Keep the tradition of it if not the rings themselves."

"Oh, I like that idea. Mom and Dad couldn't afford much when they got married. They only had their wedding bands for the first ten years, then Dad bought her the engagement and eternity rings after Shelby was born and their family was complete."

"I want you to tell me all about them. Do you have photo albums? Pa has a stack of them from when I was younger. I'm sure he'd be thrilled to show them to you when we head back to Baton Rouge."

"I'd like that, and yes, I have a storage facility full of my parents' things. I didn't want to go through it all without Shelby, and she's been avoiding it for years."

"How long is it since they died?" I know the answer; it was in the PI's report, but I want to hear it from Walker. I want him to tell me all the personal details I would learn as our relationship developed.

"Seven years. Shel was two months shy of eighteen, four months from heading to college. They'd gone for a weekend away. A drunk driver took them out on their way home."

I tighten my arms around him. "I'm sorry."

"Me too. They would have liked you."

"I'm sure the feeling would be mutual."

"I hope so."

"I know so. They made you and Shelby, didn't they?"

He huffs a laugh. "Only the best parts."

"They're all great parts, Walker."

"I'm not sure about that. My judgment has not been the best in the past when it comes to women."

"And I'd have to say the same for myself when it comes to men."

His arms around me tighten. "We've got it right now, though."

"Yeah, I think we do."

We're still wrapped in each other's arms when Blake interrupts us.

"Is it okay to give my brothers your address, Walker? They've got a possible lead on our hot shot."

"You still haven't told me who you're hunting." He removes one arm from around me and turns us both to face Blake who gives us a look because we're still on our knees.

She must decide it's not worth a question because the next words out of her mouth are, "Lattimer. Branton Lattimer."

I feel the jolt go through Walker. I know what he's thinking. I've got the same reservations but unlike me he doesn't immediately reject the idea.

Blake drills me with her gaze. "And don't you start. I know what you think."

"I've read the report. We all have."

"Yes. But that's all bare bones facts and doesn't take into account the human factor."

"He turned up to a game drunk—"

"Again." Blake puts up a hand. "I don't want to hear it. Not until you've met him."

"What's the lead your brother has?"

"Brothers, plural. The twins think he's living at a friend's place in—"

"Parry Sound," Walker finishes for her.

"You know where he is?"

"Yeah, the place he's staying belongs to Gannon."

"Gannon Byrd?"

"Yes."

Blake shakes her head. "Dammit. I told those shitheads I'd owe them a favor if they came through for me and all I had to do was ask you."

I grin at her. "They're going to make you do the ice dip again, aren't they?"

She shivers, a full body shake that rattles her teeth. "Fuckers."

Moving away from Walker, I stand and head in her direction. "C'mon, you know you love it once it's over."

"Yeah, I love that it's over. It's the one part of the training our dad taught us I hate."

"But your dad loves it when you all do it."

"He does. But the twins usually find an excuse to not do it, same as me. It's only Mason and Sutton that love it and turned it into a holiday tradition."

"Well, why don't we put our heads together and find a way to trick the twins into doing it with you."

"I can't think of anything."

"I can."

We both turn to face Walker, who's also gotten to his feet.

"By now they've heard about the Rogues, right?"

"Yeah, they told me I was an idiot for asking about Branton."

He nods. "I expect so. But here's the thing. I'm with you. I think he'd be a key player. We haven't talked about that yet, but I have watched your career, I know the family you come from, and I know and have played with Branton."

"Okay, how's that going to get the twins to—"

"We play to their egos."

"Oh, I see where you're going with this," I say. "We bet the Rogues beat them the first time we play. Or that our hot shot can score more points than them in the season or—"

"Exactly." Walker comes over and puts his hand out toward Blake. "I'll make you a deal. If we can't get your brothers, hell even if we can, I'll do the ice dip with you."

"Why would you want to do that?"

"Because you and I are a team and you put yourself out there for our team."

She eyes him and I'm about to interject when she grabs his hand.

"Deal." After they shake, Blake adds, "Dad is gonna love this."

"For a chance to meet Andrew Watts, I'd gladly volunteer."

"You're a fan?"

"What self-respecting hockey fan or player isn't?" Walker counters.

"True. True. So do I tell the twins I don't need them to come here? They said something about taking me to the owner of the place they think Branton is at."

"The owner shares an apartment with my sister."

"Oh. Right. Gannon." Blake glances at me and I give a hopefully subtle shake of my head. "If you can get the address, we can head to see Branton after you two get married. Are we going to Vegas for that?"

"I was thinking of seeing if Pa could organize something at home. Maybe the back garden of the house."

"Oh, yes, that would be gorgeous and it's a good time of year for a wedding in the south." Blake grins.

"I'd like everyone there and I know Cami is champing at the bit to get home."

"She hates the city. Any big city."

I nod. "I know. I can't work out how Pa got her here."

"He reminded her that the four of us are in this together."

"I don't think she forgets."

"No. But she does try to escape whenever she can."

"She's always been that way. I had to badger her into being friends when Fenton brought her home."

Blake laughs. "I remember. I swear, you pestered her until she rolled over."

"I'll get her in on this too."

"Don't push her. She'll come around. Once she sees the frenzy from the fans, her insatiable curiosity of human nature will make her want to study every aspect of the team, game, fans, she won't be able to help herself."

"I'm counting on it."

"Maybe you could play to her journalist side?" Walker offers.

"I tried that."

"But now you actually have the team and the public knows about it, and the next few weeks, hell months, are going to ramp things up."

"True. I wanted her to do a behind-the-scenes thing."

"She still could," Blake says.

"She could." I ponder the possibilities, but I know I probably won't get my wish until we're closer to playing in the league. Which means I've got over a year to wear her down. It took me less than that to convince her to be my friend.

"C'mon, food should be arriving any minute and I need to

make a call to see about our hot shot." Walker places his hand on my lower back and urges me out of the room. "I also need to call Shelby. Let her know what we decided."

"Oh, did we decide?" I ask.

"Yeah, I think so. I really like the idea of each of us having a piece of our parents' happy marriage to carry forward."

Blake side-eyes me so I say, "His parents' rings."

"Ah." She nods. "I'll call my brothers, let them know not to bother coming over."

"They can if you want to see them while you're here." Walker offers as we enter the living room to find Cami and Nat facing off.

"What's going on?"

"Dickhead rang," Cami spits. She's the one who least favors Nat's husband and isn't shy about letting everyone know.

"What did he want?" Blake asks retaking her seat on the couch.

"A job." Nat sighs. "I know you all don't like him. I get why."

"I wish you'd tell us why you're still married to him." I don't voice my thoughts on the man or her reluctance to divorce him but I do want to understand why.

"I won't be after the new year."

Cami is out of her chair. "What? You're divorcing him?"

"Yes." Nat rubs at her forehead. "I have the evidence I need to make sure he can't touch any of my personal wealth and we made sure long ago that he can't touch Rogue or the Rogues."

"What evidence? You've always been so tight lipped about the two of you."

"Because the marriage was never my idea. I did it to gain access to my trust funds."

"Wow." Cami sinks back into her chair. "Why didn't you tell us?"

"Because I knew as soon as I said I do that I'd made a mistake and it's been easy to keep my life separate from his. Most of the time."

"What do you need from us?" I move to her, sit beside her,

and place an arm around her shoulders. "Whatever you need, it's yours."

"Patience."

"He's going to be a dick, isn't he?"

"He already is, why would he change now? Especially when Nat is taking away his money vault." Blake slips her arm around Nat from her other side. "Can I be there when you boot him out?"

"I'm giving him the house."

"What?" Cami is on her feet again. "Why?"

"It's easier. Plus I never liked it. I'm moving into an apartment in our complex for now. It'll suit me better, being close to the arena. And let's be real, I've been pretty much living in the company apartment for months."

She had. I hadn't thought too much about it because we've been so busy building the new manufacturing facility as well as bidding on the franchise. I figured with all the late nights and the fact we've all, except for Cami, spent a number of nights in the apartment each week, it was convenient.

Now I see it was her way of moving away from Johnathon sooner than she officially could.

"When are you serving him the papers?" I ask. "Is this going to cause a problem for the Rogues?"

"Before the phone call I would have said no. Now I'm not so sure. I need to think about it, talk to him next week when he gets back from Europe."

"When did he go to Europe?"

"Last month. He's staying in the chalet. Skiing."

I can't stop the bark of laughter from bursting out. It isn't long before the others join in.

Walker eyes us all. "Why is him skiing funny?"

"Because he's the least coordinated man on the planet. Last summer he broke his nose surfing."

"Yeah, about that. He wasn't surfing when he broke it. He

was hitting on his instructor and her husband didn't take too kindly to that," Nat explains.

"Oh my god, that just makes it funnier." Blake puts her hands up in a prayer position. "Please tell me all the other injuries occurred the same way."

Nat shrugs. "Don't know. I've only been having him followed for the last few years."

"Followed? You've been collecting evidence for years?" I ask, still confused as to why she's waited. "That doesn't explain why you didn't do it before now."

"I couldn't do anything until after I turned thirty and all the clauses and stipulations on the family trusts became void."

"Oh. Your grandfather tied it all up until then?"

"Yes. It's why we never moved into the family home. I couldn't live there until after thirty and only if I was married. I still won't be able to live there because I won't be married in a few months."

"Jesus. This conversation needs wine. Got any wine, Walker?" Cami asks as she moves toward the kitchen. "Or maybe champagne? We do have a few things to celebrate."

She's right, we do. The Rogues contract and announcement, Nat's impending divorce, and my engagement.

The next few years are looking bright, and I can't wait to get started on them with four people who mean everything to me.

WALKER

We make the collective decision to return to Baton Rouge together. None of us want the media to get wind of a certain hot shot and with the way photographers and reports are following, calling, and getting in our faces, it makes sense to lead them all to where we want them.

The Rogues multi-million-dollar arena.

Plus there is a wedding we want to have at some point.

Soon.

I want Shelby and Gannon to be there but that's proving difficult to organize.

In the end, we put the wedding on hold and concentrate on the other things going on.

Like the press conference to announce my retirement.

The Knights graciously allow me to dictate where that will take place. Laken even offered to fly down to Baton Rouge to do it.

She's proving to be a competent team owner, although I'm sure Rafe is helping her a lot.

As much as I appreciate her offer, and because I don't want to appear as though there is any animosity between me and my old team, Oakley and I fly back to New York three days after we leave it.

The trip serves two purposes.

This morning's announcement that was completely anticlimactic after the recent days of media attention.

Laken made the announcement, shook my hand, offered me the best for the future, and I answered a few questions about what's next for me and that was it.

There was only one question about Oakley. We'd spoken about the possibility of that and decided to give them something to hopefully lessen their interest.

I confirmed our relationship and that we'd been friends for months before the friendship took a romantic turn. When someone asked about my knowledge of the Rogues, I chose to cut it there.

Surprisingly, we were left alone after that. Of course, that may have had something to do with the fact Laken had a second announcement about the Knights that put the spotlight squarely on her and my old team.

Oakley wants to stick around for a while to make sure Laken doesn't need anything which leads us to this afternoon.

And packing.

"What about this? Need any of it?" Oakley holds up a stack of dishes.

"Do I?" I have no idea where we'll be living. I'm assuming it won't be in the company apartment where we stayed the last few nights.

"Probably not. But do you want it?"

"You know..." I shut the cupboard door where my coffee mugs are. "I don't really need anything but personal items. I'm sure you've got household goods."

"I do. Although..." She looks at me uncertainly.

"What?"

"I live with Pa."

"Okay. So, it's already furnished."

"As soon as we get a chance, we'll look for somewhere to live."

"Why? You don't want to live there anymore?"

"I didn't think you would want to."

Walking over, I wrap her up in my arms. "Oak. I'll live in a box under a bridge if I get to do it with you."

"Well, we don't need to go to that extreme." She grins. "The house is big. And Pa's room in on the ground floor, far away from my room."

"Will he object to us living there? Together? He might be okay with his granddaughter living with him but adding me to the house could be a deal breaker for him."

"No. He's talking about moving out to give us the house."

"Why would he move out of his home?"

"I don't think he's serious. At least I hope not. I think maybe he thought you wouldn't want to live with him."

"Huh. I guess I need to make it clear I'm not about to usurp his place in your life and home."

"Funnily enough, I think he might want you to. I think he's hoping for great grandchildren."

"I'm ready to give him those whenever you are," I tell her.

"You... I..." She shakes her head, and I have to smile that I've managed to make her speechless. It's not something easily done.

I'll be honest, I haven't given kids much thought, but I do know I want them.

"I know we've got a lot going on. We don't need to add to the chaos right now but when you're ready, I'm game."

"We're not even married yet?" she argues. Although we're not fighting because as I said, whenever she wants them is fine with me.

I shrug. "I'm not worried about that."

"You're not one of those men who needs the mother of his children to bear his name?"

"No. Do I want you to? Yes. Need you to? No. Besides, I thought you'd want to keep your maiden name."

"James?"

"Yes."

"Why?"

"It's your family name and I know you're the last of your line to pass it on."

"Right, well, it's actually not my birth name."

"Sorry, what?"

"My mother was Pa's daughter. My father's name is Doyle. When Pa came and got me, he had my last name changed to James."

I'm so surprised by this information that I don't speak for several seconds. But then something occurs to me that I can't believe I haven't noticed before now. "You don't talk about your parents. At all."

"No. My mother died when I was two and my father didn't want me after that and didn't take care of me very well. Pa and Grams came and got me when I was three. I've lived with them since."

She hasn't mentioned her grandmother before either and I have a feeling I know the answer to my next question but ask anyway. "Grams?"

"My grandmother. She died when I was twenty-two."

Saying sorry in these situations always seems useless so I go with something else. "I wish I'd gotten to meet her. She raised an amazing woman."

"I have no idea where I would be if they hadn't come for me. Probably dead in a gutter like my father."

"Wait. Your father is dead?"

"Yes, he was walking home drunk and got hit by a car. Grams said it was a blessing because after my mother died, he turned into someone she didn't recognize, someone she didn't like."

I tighten my arms around her for a second before letting go and palming her face. Lowering my head, I bring our lips together in a quick kiss. "There's so much about each other we don't know."

"We've got time."

"We do, but I have the urge to rush through it all because I want to know every part of you."

"I feel the same."

"It still surprises me how much I feel for you." I press my forehead to hers. "It's all-consuming."

"Glad I'm not alone in that."

"We're a pair."

She grins. "Yes, we are."

"A perfect pair." I hate how cliché I sound but it's how I feel. She's perfect for me. She's not perfect, neither am I, but together we're a perfect fit.

"I've always known what a healthy marriage looks like because Pa and Grams had one but I never understood how they could fight like dogs one second and love on each other the next. But I get it now."

"We haven't had a fight yet."

"No. But I can't imagine not loving you through it."

"My mother used to say she knew she loved my dad completely because other than her children he was the only person on the planet that could make her want to strangle him and kiss him at the same time."

She laughs, her face still cradled in my hands, my forehead on hers. "Grams used to say something similar. She'd tell me Pa made her want to kiss and kill him in the same breath."

"Yeah, that's it exactly."

"We'll have that."

"Yes." Neither of us is questioning it. Which says more than anything how deep we both are.

I never saw myself falling in love. Yes, I've dated, screwed around too, but love has never been on my radar.

Not until a smokin' hot woman came out from behind blinding lights and metaphorically took me to my knees.

And suddenly I can't wait any longer to get on with our lives. Letting her go, I step back.

"Okay, let's pack some of my clothes so we can get back home.

As much as I want Shelby and Gannon there, I want to marry you more."

"Wait, what? You've giving me whiplash, Walker."

"Let's grab a few things and leave the rest. I can have movers come in and box everything up, ship it to Baton Rouge, and worry about it then. For now, I want to get home as quick as we can so I can reassure your Pa that if he's happy to have me living under his roof, that's where we'll be."

I grab her hand and tow her toward the bedroom.

"I also want to get married as soon as we can. We can video call Shelby and Gannon if they can't make it down."

"Oh, well, Pa has a friend who can marry us."

"He does? When do you think we can organize it?"

"If you don't want anything fancy, we could probably do it as soon as Uncle Merle is available."

"Uncle Merle?"

She shrugs. "He's married to my Grams' best friend."

"Jeez, all these people, this whole life I know nothing about. I can't wait to discover it all." Spinning her around, I tug her against my chest and press my lips to hers. "I'll never know enough about you to get bored."

I back her up to the bed and when her legs hit the mattress, I give her a little shove.

Laughing as she bounces on the bed, she pushes to her elbows and asks, "What are you doing?"

"Getting to know you better."

"I think you know me pretty well when it comes to this."

"Maybe." I pull my shirt out of my pants and over my head then grin at her wolfishly. "But I better check just to be sure."

And then I'm on her. My mouth on hers, my tongue thrusting between her lips to tangle with hers.

My hands aren't idle either. They work at her clothes until I have to break our kiss to get her naked from the waist up.

She's not wearing a bra. Why didn't I notice that before?

"No bra? All morning?"

"No, the shirt you just ripped off me has a built-in shelf bra."

I shake my head. "I don't even know what that is. And I don't care because..." I wave a hand toward her chest.

Her perfect tits are on display and in the next breath my hands get busy testing every millimeter of them. From the fullness of their curves to the weight of them in my palms to the beaded tips that beg for my mouth.

Which sounds like a fantastic idea.

Lowering my head, I suck one peak deep and press it to the roof of my mouth with my tongue. My suction is hard and the sharp breath she pulls in tells me I've hit the edge of her pain threshold.

I've toyed with her tolerance over the last week. She likes the barest edge of pain to go with her pleasure but it's a fine balance. One I'm still learning.

In spite of what she said, and what we've done together so far, I don't know her completely.

But I will.

I'll spend the rest of my life learning every little thing that turns her on. Everything that turns her off.

I'll know when to push her and when to pull back. Know when to take it fast, when to take it slow.

But most of all, I'll know she's mine.

"Walker."

Her breathless voice, the squirming of her hips, the clench of her hands in my hair, all tell me it's time to take it fast.

In seconds I have us both stripped naked and I'm lying over her, my weight supported by my arms.

"I'm going to love you so hard."

The smile she gives me is all sass. "Can you do it now or are you waiting for an invitation?"

"Minx."

I cut off anything else she might say with my mouth on hers. I take the kiss deep, push it hard, and while I've got her distracted with my mouth I wiggle my way deeper between her legs until the hot wet flesh I've explored again and again is pressing along the length of my cock.

The groan that leaves me is guttural. It's pain and pleasure and the end of my plan to explore her more because in that moment my restraint snaps.

With a hard stab, I impale her slick heat with my hard dick.

A cry leaves her throat and for half a second I panic, but then she rocks up into me, claws at my shoulders, my back, and I'm left with no concern I've hurt her in my rush.

"Oak." I search for her mouth again.

I love kissing her, as much as I love fucking her.

The two together blow my mind.

Then again, it's Oakley who does that just by breathing.

Together we rock and roll and it's only a few minutes later that I'm gritting my teeth in an attempt to hold off my release.

But that fucker is barreling toward me like a defenseman on the ice in the final seconds of a tied-up Cup game.

Except I'm not about to get slammed into the boards.

Not before she does.

Lifting up on my hands I shift the angle of penetration and am rewarded with the most delicious sound and clench.

The cry is one of blissed relief, the clench a hot grip capturing my cock inside her.

Her orgasm sucks her under and drags me along behind. I can't stop my release even if I want to. And I don't.

Coming together, reaching that peak and shooting off it at the same time is the most pleasurable experience I've ever had, and I held the fucking Cup!

But this, Oakley under me, me inside her, both of us lost to the pleasure coming together brings is the highlight of my life.

I have no idea how we top this. If we can.

Well, not without dying anyway.

Panting for breath, I slump on top of her and wonder if I haven't just come as close to death as anyone can get and still be alive.

"Walker."

"Sorry." I move us to our sides, keeping us joined, but take my weight off her.

"That's not what I was trying to tell you."

"Oh?" My brain is buzzing and I'm not sure if it's lack of oxygen or if our climaxes destroyed my ear drums.

"Your phone."

"Huh?" I lift my head and look at a very mussed Oakley. "My phone?"

"It's going crazy in the other room."

Tilting my head I try to listen but the drum of my heart is hard to hear over. How she's capable of hearing is beyond—

The buzzing starts up again and I realize it's not my brain making that sound.

"Shit. That's the door. Which means whoever is on the other side has access to the building."

Not wanting to leave her but knowing I've got no choice, I disengage our bodies to the sound of our mutual disappointment. "I know," I soothe, "We'll get back to this after I tell whoever that is to fuck off."

She laughs as she rolls off the bed. "It's probably Shelby."

"Again?" Although I am impressed she hasn't just used her key to come in. "Huh. Guess she learned not to barge in after the other day."

"She's showing both of us respect. Before I came along, she had unlimited access to her brother. Now she knows that's no longer the case and being respectful because of it."

"You give her too much credit. She's probably just forgotten the pass code."

"I'll go let her in." Oakley pulls my discarded shirt over her head.

"The hell you will! Not dressed like that. I'll go." I hop into my pants as I head out of the room.

By the time I get to the front door my pants are done up and the buzzer is going again.

"I'm coming!" Twisting the lock, I grab the handle and yank the door open. "This better be—"

My words are cut off as Shelby, followed by a grim-faced Gannon push inside.

"She's all over the internet, says the kid is yours, and you're refusing to take responsibility for him."

"Who is? What kid?" I close the door and turn to face my sister.

Shelby shoves her phone in my face, but I can't focus on the screen before she pulls it away and yells.

"Kristina and the little boy who looks like a mini you!"

OAKLEY

"He's not mine," Walker says for the millionth time. "He can't be mine."

"I know."

He's pacing behind me, his reflection crossing my screen every few seconds, but soothing him is the last thing I can do because I'm busy working out who the little boy Kristina is claiming belongs to Walker is.

"I didn't even know she had a kid."

"She doesn't," I say.

"The pictures prove otherwise," he counters.

"They prove nothing other than she's spent time with a toddler recently."

"Fuck!" He stops behind me and slams the fingers of both hands through his hair, tugs on the ends.

"Walker." When that doesn't get his attention, I leave my chair and my laptop and step in front of him. "Walker!"

"What? Sorry." He wraps his arms around me and pulls me against his chest. "She's a liar."

"I know she is. And I'm pretty sure I can get to the bottom of this if you calm down and let me."

"I can't have a kid with her. I can't. She's…" He squeezes me tightly, the sound of his hard swallow filling my ear. "I can't."

"You don't. I'm not sure what's going on here, but I know, in my gut, that little boy isn't yours."

"Fuck. It sounds horrible, but I hope to hell you're right."

"I am. You'll see. But first you need to take a breath and calm down. Let me do what I need to so you can stop worrying."

"First Cantrell's bullshit, now this. You shouldn't have to deal with my shit, Oak."

"When I said yes, it became our shit."

The sigh that leaves him has his whole body softening against me. "I love you," he murmurs into my hair.

Smiling, I pinch his waist, not that there's much to pinch. The man doesn't have anything but lean muscle covering every inch of him. "That's not why I'm helping."

"Why then?"

"Because I love you and no one, and I mean *no one*, least of all some hockey wife wanna be, fucks with what's mine."

"I kinda get hard when you go all bloodthirsty," he whispers into my ear. "Don't move or my sister and best friend are going to see just how much."

Glancing over my shoulder I see Shelby and Gannon talking in low tones. They haven't done anything obvious but because I know they're together I see it. I understand how Walker doesn't though. And I'm not about to enlighten him.

"You two going to stick around for dinner?" I ask. It will help keep Walker sane to hang out with his best friend and sister.

"Do you want us to?" Shelby moves away from Gannon.

"Yes. We're heading back to Baton Rouge tomorrow morning so if you can stay it would be great because I don't know when we'll get to do it again."

"Sure. Okay. Want me to order in?" She holds up her phone.

"Yes, help Walker decide what to get and distract him long enough for me to find the information I need to discredit Kristina's claims."

"I don't understand what she's trying to do. If the kid is Walker's, she would have gotten pregnant when they first met and there's plenty of pictures of her and him together during that first year and she isn't pregnant in any of them."

"There's that. But there's also the fact she's never been seen in public with the child before now, and that's only been in the pictures online, and that one article said her neighbors are saying she doesn't have a child living with her and never has."

"That's the other thing. Where has he been for...what, two, three years?"

"He looks about three to me," Gannon adds.

He hasn't spoken much since they arrived. I can't decide if that's his usual state or if he's wary of me. "I agree. Which means Shelby is right—she would have been pregnant the first year Walker was an idiot."

That makes everyone laugh, which was my intent. We need to lighten the mood in here. I can't believe I'm once again dealing with the ridiculousness of other people.

First Jerry tried to fuck with me by leaking the information about the franchise, and now Kristina.

Although I shouldn't be surprised. Those two *are* in bed together.

While Shelby and Gannon distract Walker, I head to the bedroom and place a call to the PI I have on retainer.

The man has contacts the likes of which I do not want to know but they serve me well so I'll continue to turn a blind eye to any less than legal means of information collection he may use.

"Hey, Oakley, what can I do for you today?"

"Hi, Amos. I need you to do a little digging for me."

"Sure. Who?"

"You've worked on her before, Kristina Bancroft."

"If I've worked her up already, why am I doing it again?"

"Because this afternoon she's all over the internet with a child she's claiming is the son of my fiancé."

"Fiancé? That's new?"

"Last week. Walker Alcott."

"Ah, right. Okay, what exactly do you want me to find?"

"Birth certificate? The kid's name? I don't know. All I know is he can't be Walker's son because she would have been pregnant the first year they were together for that to be true."

"Are you sure? How old is the kid?"

"He looks about three."

"Yeah, if I'm remembering right, she couldn't have hidden a pregnancy while they were first together. Are you sure he's that old?"

"Yes. I'll send you a link to one of the articles—"

"Don't bother, I'll dig around and see what I can find and get back to you."

"Thanks, Amos." Hanging up, I lower my phone and stare out the windows, not really seeing the city before me.

"Who was that?"

I turn to see Walker leaning against the wall just inside the bedroom door. "PI."

"Ah, okay." He pushes off the wall and stalks toward me. "You have no idea how much I want to fuck you right now."

"Because I've got my PI investigating Kristina's latest grab for fame?"

"You think that's what she's doing?" He stops in front of me but doesn't reach out.

"Yes. Although I thought she was a little smarter than this. It's going to be so easy to discredit her claim. I've already got a timeline of pictures taken the first two years you were with her and there isn't even a bump to her belly."

He moves in, lifts his hands, and cradles my face. "You do me in, Oakley."

"Is that good or bad?"

"Good and bad." He grins.

"Oh?"

"Good because you own me. I'm yours one hundred percent. And bad because you're not getting rid of me now."

Pressing his mouth to mine, he pauses there, our lips barely connected. I want more but he's obviously got an agenda or he'd have dived deep already.

"I wish I could give you half of what you give me."

"You do. The feelings go both ways, Walker."

"Yes, but you're bailing me out of every—"

I pull back and slap my palm over his mouth. "This is not a one-for-one deal. It's balance, and sometimes one of us holds more than the other. It's the only way a true partnership works, and I think that's what we've got, what we're building, right?"

He pulls my hand away to speak. "I'd like to think so. But I can't help wondering when you're going to get sick of me bringing all the crazy to your life."

I smile. "I'm going to remind you of this conversation when the shoe is on the other foot because it will be once we start pushing the Rogues."

"I'm here for whatever you need."

"And if I need you to kiss me?"

"Just say when."

"When."

He doesn't disappoint me. His lips are on mine, his tongue sweeping back and forth in a slow caress that has me wishing we could head back to bed.

But even as I think that, he's retreating. When he lets my mouth go completely, he rests his forehead on mine and cradles my face the way he likes to do, the way I like him to.

"We ordered Chinese."

"Okay." The change of topic seems weird except I think I know what he's doing. He's bringing us both back from the edge so we don't tumble onto the bed. I can help with that. "Are we setting the table or eating in the living room?"

"Table. Shelby is on it. Gannon is checking on our hot shot."

"He left?"

"No, he's giving him a call, pretending it's just to check up on the house, but it's to see if he's still there."

"You haven't explained how Branton came to be staying at Gannon's place."

"It's been empty since Gannon's grandma passed four years ago. When Branton wanted a place to lick his wounds, Gannon offered. He's been there since he walked away from the league."

"Over a year, right?"

"Yeah. I'm not sure if he'll want what we're offering."

"I'm not worried about that. I want to know if he can do what we're asking."

"Yes." He lifts his head, his gaze locking on mine. "He's the best in the league—"

"Was."

"No. *Is*. I'd lay money on it."

"Really?"

"Yes. He may have turned up drunk to a game but he'd never done it before. Never been one of the partiers of the game either. I don't think that would have changed. I could be wrong, I know that, but my gut tells me I'm not. Not when it comes to Branton Lattimer."

"I hope you're right. Blake thinks he's what we need. Which reminds me, I've got some names and files for you to read."

"Blake said you had a list already."

"Only those that aren't playing right now. We've got time, but if we're pulling in ex-players or those who haven't played in the league yet we want to get the—to use a hockey term—puck moving early."

"Is that a hockey term?" He grins at me.

With a shrug I say, "I don't know but you know what I mean."

"You're cute." He bops the end of my nose with a fingertip. "Get the puck moving early." Chuckling, he shakes his head and slings his arm around my shoulders to guide me out of the room.

"You'll have to teach me the right terms."

"Blake hasn't done that?"

"Some. But that part of the game isn't something I've spent too much time learning."

"Don't worry, I'll catch you up."

"I'm counting on it."

"You can count on me for whatever you need." Placing a kiss on my forehead, he adds. "Now go help Shel set the table while I talk with Gannon to see what his thoughts are on Branton."

"Oh, look at you in coach mode."

He puts his arms out and says, "Good look, right?"

He's in the pants he yanked on when his sister and best friend knocked on the door. He's added a shirt, an old workout shirt that's full of holes and stains of lord knows what.

He shouldn't look hot. And maybe to someone else he wouldn't, but me? I'm salivating and the thought of the bare flesh hiding behind his zipper has me thinking about the bedroom we just left.

Dropping his arms, he growls, "Don't look at me like that."

I raise one eyebrow.

"Not if you don't want me dragging you back to the bedroom and locking the door behind us."

Is it bad that I like the effect I have on him? Probably. I should at least wait until we're alone to give him the look.

Attempting to clear my face of any desire, I hold up my hands. "I'll behave."

"Not all the time I hope," he mutters with a shake of his head.

"Lady on the streets, freak in the sheets?"

"What?" he chokes out on a laugh. "Fuck, woman. You never fail to surprise me."

"It's good to be unpredictable. Keeping people on their toes is a good thing."

"I'm not on my toes with you, I'm on my knees."

Before I can comment, Shelby interrupts us.

"If you two are finished making fuck-me eyes at each other, dinner's here."

We're both grinning like idiots as soon as she leaves the hallway.

"C'mon. Let's have dinner before it gets cold. I can talk to Gannon about Branton later."

"You're not going to tell him why you want to know about him?"

"Oh, I kind of did but not specifically. Just asked him to check in with the guy to see if he's still hanging in there and when I ask him about what his thoughts are on Bran's abilities, it'll be as one player to another. Gannon doesn't know about the job." He whispers the last part in my ear.

"Oh." I hadn't thought about that.

Now that the league has announced the team my brain has switched from secret mode, except some things still need to be kept from the public, and while I'm sure Walker's best friend is trustworthy, I'm not sure I want to reveal who the Rogues have acquired as head coach.

Especially seeing how we don't have a signed contract yet.

Something I will rectify the minute we return to Rogues headquarters.

"Everything okay, Oakley?" Shelby asks.

"Oh, yes, sorry, I was mentally running through my to-do list for tomorrow."

"What time are you leaving?"

"We're on a seven am flight."

"I wish we had more time together, but I know you must have a ton of stuff to do." She grabs my arm. "Did I tell you how excited I am about the Rogues? I love that you ladies are taking on the world of hockey."

I do a quick memory-bank check to recall what I've told Shelby about the team. I know she has no clue her brother will be head coach, and I'm pretty sure the only thing she knows is the women behind Rogue sportswear are behind the franchise.

"It was a long time coming. It feels great to be able to talk about it."

"I've followed KAW since my first year of college. I had to do a report on a successful business that's embracing sustainable practices and your solar powered manufacturing facilities intrigued me."

"We've still got a way to go on those but we're at sixty percent self-sufficient at present."

"I wish I'd known you when I had to do my report. I could have picked your brain for all the details."

"You could have emailed any one of us. We'd have been glad to help you."

"Oh, I did. Natalie Redding was really great. She found someone in the organization to answer all my questions."

"Good. I'm glad you got what you needed, but if you're ever curious about either business, let me know."

"I will."

"Ready to eat? I'm starving." Walker nudges his sister with his shoulder. "Gannon's already at the table. If we don't get in there soon, he'll eat it all."

Shelby laughs. "He's not that bad."

There are subtle signs when a woman is in love with a man and not wanting anyone to know. I see them in Shelby. I'm not sure why they're hiding their relationship; it's been going on for years if the PI's report is accurate.

How Walker hasn't gotten suspicious is beyond me. Then again, if you're not looking for something, you tend not to see it. I'll just have to be ready for when they do announce their relationship.

I'm sure there will be some fallout. They've both lied by omission for years. That's going to hurt Walker no matter how he feels about his best friend and little sister getting together.

"What do you want to drink with dinner? I've got wine."

"Water. I don't want to open a bottle for one glass. With us returning to Baton Rouge tomorrow, it'll go to waste."

"Good point. Water it is. Be right back."

I watch him head for the kitchen when the front door buzzer fills the apartment. "I'll get it!"

I leave Shelby and Gannon quietly arguing over what to eat and head for the door. Opening it, I find Henry on the doorstep.

"Ah, Ms. James." He glances behind me. "Is Mr. Alcott in?"

"He is, do you need him?"

"Um, yeah." He glances to the side. "Someone left him a...package."

I tilt my head quizzically. I'm not sure why he's being guarded. We've met several times now. "Can I take it?"

"Um, no." He straightens. "I think it best if you get Mr. Alcott."

I nod but I don't get a chance to turn before a sound has me leaning forward and peering to the left.

The breath I suck in gets caught in my throat.

Big gray-blue eyes stare up at me. Eyes identical to the ones I've spent hours looking into.

Shelby is right.

As much as we know it can't be true, the little boy in front of me is the spitting image of the man in the apartment behind me.

WALKER

"I don't understand," I whisper in Oakley's ear so the boy doesn't hear me. "How do you just leave a kid on someone's doorstep?"

"I don't know. I'm trying to work out what her game is."

"We have to call the police." I don't want to. The kid looks lost. And scared. He hasn't said a word since he came inside.

He didn't even utter a sound, just nodded his head, when Oakley offered him ice cream.

"I don't think we should do that yet."

My gaze darts to her. "Why?" I flinch at the volume of my voice, my eyes going back to the quiet little boy at the end of the table.

He doesn't seem as though my near shout even registered. Is he used to people yelling around him?

God. I have so many questions. The first, how the hell does this kid look so much like me!?

Shelby and Gannon took off right after Henry delivered our guest to get supplies for a toddler. I have no idea what those supplies might be but I'm grateful someone is doing something.

"We need to find out his name." Oakley pushes out of her chair and heads over to him.

Wary eyes watch her, zip to me then back again. His tiny body

201

is braced, for what I don't know, but if I find out someone has been mistreating this kid…

"Hey." She crouches beside his chair. "You remember my name is Oakley and that's Walker, right?"

She gets a nod. Not really progress because we received one of those when the ice cream was offered.

"What should we call you?" she asks softly. "Do you have a nickname? Walker calls me Oak but I used to get OJ when I was little because my full name is Oakley James."

"Micky." His voice is so quiet I barely hear him and can't help moving closer, but I stop the instant he jerks back and fearful eyes meet mine.

Fuck! Some motherfucker has scared this kid!

"Is that a nickname?" I ask softly hoping to ease his worry.

He shakes his head, but his eyes don't leave me. It takes all my restraint to keep my fingers from curling into fists. The terrified look on the boy's face makes me want to punch something.

Someone.

"Okay, Micky. Do you know your mom's name?" Oakley continues the questions.

Another shake of his head with eyes locked on me.

How does he not know his mother's name? Then again, he'd call her Mom or Mommy, right? He's still young.

"It's my birthday next week, I'll be thirty-three," Oakley says. "And Walker's birthday is next month. He'll be twenty-nine. How old are you, Micky?"

He holds up three tiny fingers.

"Three? You're so big! I bet you go to school, yeah?"

He shakes his head again and in the last few minutes his little shoulders have relaxed and he's no longer looking at me as though I'm going to beat him with a stick.

"Do you know where you live?"

Before he can answer, Oakley's phone rings. Glancing at the screen, I see the name Amos. "It's the PI."

"I need to answer my phone. Will you be okay if I go over

there and talk to the person calling me?" She doesn't move until Micky nods.

Then she pushes to her feet and looks at his bowl. The one half filled with melting ice cream.

"Would you like something else to eat?" she asks as her phone goes silent.

Micky shakes his head then pushes the bowl away so he can rest his forearms on the table and lower his chin to them.

He looks so sad it breaks my heart. I don't know where this kid came from and I don't know what his circumstances are, but I need him to be okay. And if I have to step in to make that happen, I will.

Oakley moves back to me and scoops up her phone. "I'll stay in sight," she whispers.

Like Micky, all I can do is nod.

And listen.

"Hey, Amos. Sorry about that. We've got some unexpected company."

I don't hear what the man says but I do see the crease in her brow as she listens to him, her eyes on me.

"Are you sure?"

She's nodding now, her gaze darting between me and Micky.

"Okay. He's here. I'm not sure if we should call the..." her words trail off when her eyes land on Micky as he climbs out of his chair and hides under the table. "Ah, Amos? Can you get those documents to me? Anything else you can dig up too?"

I can only imagine the man has found the boy's birth certificate. I hope so. We need to know who his parents are so we can work out whether to take him to them or keep him hidden under my dining table.

"Thanks. Bye." Coming back to me, she keeps an eye on the other end of the table as she bends down to whisper in my ear. "Do you have a cousin? Michael?"

"Yeah, but we haven't seen him since my dad's brother took

off with him back when we were…shit, I think I was ten. Why? Is Micky his?"

"The paperwork says so."

"So how'd he get here?"

"Michael was killed in a car accident a couple of months ago."

"Oh." I should be saddened but I don't feel anything but confused. I have my cousin's little boy and no idea how.

"Amos is going to keep digging but it appears as though your cousin left you his son."

"What?" I can't stop myself from jackknifing out of my seat. A small whimper from under the table has me immediately cursing myself. "*Oak.*"

I don't know what I'm trying to say. I have nothing in my head but the fear I see in Micky's eyes every time he looks at me. Was my cousin a child abuser?

I shove my fingers through my hair and grip the back of my head. "What do we do?"

"We find out how to keep him."

The fierceness in her voice has my gaze locking with hers. "Keep him?"

"Yes. I don't care how he came to be here, he's not leaving. I want to remove that fear I see in his eyes. I want to make him smile. What three-year-old doesn't smile at a bowl of ice cream?" she whispers urgently.

"I don't know. I haven't had much to do with kids."

"Well, Amos found a will leaving you guardianship of Michael junior so we shouldn't have any issues keeping him with us. I need to call my lawyer and we need to get married as soon as we can, or get me made co-guardian or something."

She's thinking. I can see her brain working all the angles, considering all the possibilities. "God. I didn't think I could love you any more."

"Let's see if we can coax him out from under there with a movie or cartoon or whatever it is kids watch on TV."

"I'll message Shelby, ask her to get some toys...maybe some cars or LEGOs?"

"Good idea. Why don't you go see what you can find for him to watch and I'll get him out from under there."

"I'm worried about his reaction to me."

"Oh?"

"Yeah, he's not as scared of you as he is of me."

"I did notice that but I think it's just that you're so big."

"Maybe."

"Don't think the worst. Wait until we have the facts."

I know she's right. I shouldn't assume my cousin is the reason for Micky's fear. It could be whoever he's spent the last few months with. "Where's he been since Michael died?"

"I don't know. That's one of the things Amos is looking into."

"Okay. I'll message Shel and see what I can find on Netflix."

"Thanks. And Walker?"

"Yeah."

"I love you too." She pushes to her toes and kisses me quick.

It says a lot about the situation that the peck that would normally get my motor revving doesn't even turn it over.

While I head to the living room, I send Shelby and Gannon a message asking for whatever toys they can find suitable for a three year old. Then I turn the TV on and pull up the kids section of my streaming service.

I pick the first thing on the most popular list and seconds after the theme song plays through the surround sound system, a blur of motion races into the room and drops to the floor right in front of my hundred-inch screen.

He's too close but I'm not about to tell him to move back because on his face is the one thing that could stop me from doing anything.

Make me *do* anything.

His little mouth is stretched wide in a smile that shows off tiny teeth and he's quietly singing along, bouncing on his butt.

"That was easier than I thought," Oakley says as she moves next to me. "Oh."

"Yeah."

"Okay, so we know how to get him to smile now."

I can't take my eyes off him. I should be comfortable with this instant love thing after Oakley but I'm not. The emotions I'm feeling for a child I've never seen, never knew existed, are breath-stealing.

"We can't let them take him."

"Who?"

"I don't know. Anyone. Whoever the hell has had him since…" I swallow, my throat tight, my chest aching.

Is that why I feel so connected to Micky? We're both orphans? Hell, I don't know where his mother is, if she's dead like his father.

I don't understand why this is the first I'm hearing about him. Or what Kristina's involvement is. How are there pictures of her and Micky going back months?

"What's Kristina's connection? There has to be one. All those photos…"

"I don't know but we'll find out. I'll keep Amos on it until every stone is turned over. Until we know he's safe."

"If I was named guardian, then he stays here. He'll be safe."

"In theory, yes, but I don't know what Kristina's connection is to all of this and if that poses a threat to him. To you."

"How could it be threat to him? Me?"

"I…" Her mouth snaps shut. "I don't want to speculate."

"It's me. Speculate."

"I'm worried her connection to him is the same as yours."

It takes me a minute to understand what she's getting at. "You think she's co-guardian?"

Nodding, she rolls her lips into her mouth, I assume to keep other words from tumbling out.

"Say it."

"If she is, we are going to have to fight her in court to have him removed from her care."

"What care? Henry said the only thing—" I frantically glance around. "Where's the bag he had?"

"In the foyer." She's already moving in that direction.

I follow, comfortable leaving Micky alone for a moment. Retrieving his bag, we check all the pockets, tip it upside down and give it a shake to be sure we've emptied it completely.

"It's just clothes."

"And not clean ones," I note. "I'll throw them in the washer."

"He'll need more. There's no pjs. See if Shelby and Gannon are still at the store."

"I'm texting Gannon now. What else does he need? Toothbrush? Paste?" I look up. "Or can he use ours?"

"I have no clue, but if they can find a kids one, that would be better."

"Okay." I'm typing away. "What else?"

"I don't know."

"All right. Let's get these in the wash then see if we can get anything else out of him about where he's been. You said Michael died a few months ago. How many?"

"Amos didn't give me specifics."

"Right. I guess all we can do is wait. Should we see if he'll eat something?"

"He barely touched the ice cream. Maybe wait until Shelby and Gannon get back?"

"Good idea. Shit." I scrub a hand over my jaw and note I need a shave. "I'll have to tell Shelby."

"Oh."

"And find out why this is the first I'm hearing about Michael's death or his son. And where's the boy's mother?" So many questions.

Oakley shrugs and steps up to me. Slips her arms around me. "I know you're worried but he's here now, he's safe, and we'll make sure he stays that way."

"I'm sorry. This is more crazy I'm bringing to your life."

Smiling up at me, she says, "I love your kind of crazy."

"Thank fuck for that. I have no idea what I'd be doing right now without you."

"You'd work it out."

"After I punched a few holes in walls or someone's face."

"Maybe. But I doubt it. You're not the violent type."

My gaze goes in the direction of the living room. "I can think of two reasons I'd get violent without thought."

The theme song for the show Micky is watching echoes through the apartment. "Did you put that on continuous play?" Oakley asks.

"I think so. But let's go check. You can sit with him while I get this stuff in the wash."

"You don't want to sit with him?"

"I think we need to let him get comfortable with me first."

"He might not actually be afraid of you. It might be that you look like his dad. I'm assuming you and your cousin must have looked alike, considering Micky looks so much like you."

"We did when we were younger. I have no idea if that carried through to adulthood though."

"I'm thinking it did." She pulls out of my arms. "You get the wash on and have a look in the kitchen to see if there are any snacks in there we can entice Micky with."

"I think I've got popcorn. Wait. Can a three-year-old eat popcorn?"

Oakley grabs my face and holds me still. "Don't panic. I'll google what three-year-olds eat while you wash his clothes."

"Okay. I'm okay."

"Of course, you are."

A thought occurs to me. "You realize if I am his guardian, we're going to be parents a hell of a lot quicker than either of us imagined."

"Do you think Shelby might want to take him?"

"What? No. Why would you ask that? She just finished college."

"I know. And I hate to admit I even had the thought but she's his...*second cousin?*...and a woman and..." She shrugs.

"Oh, right. Yeah, maybe. I guess I'll give her that option if I can, but if Michael named me as his guardian, then it's me, right?"

"Yes."

"Good." I nod. "Good."

She watches me closely and whatever she sees makes her smile grow bigger.

"What?"

"You're gonna be a great dad."

"This is not how I saw that happening. But if I'm a dad, you'll be a mom."

"I...*oh*." For a moment her face is blank then the most beautiful thing happens. Her eyes sparkle and her smile stretches wide. "I'll be a mom."

I cradle her face and bring our foreheads together. "Fuck, Oak. Can we do this?"

"We have to. There's no choice. He's not going back wherever he's been. No one just drops a child off in the foyer of an apartment building and gets to have him back."

The fierceness in her voice makes me smile. And then I think about what I'd like to do with whoever brought Micky here. The rage that rolls through me boils my blood and rattles my bones.

A few hours ago I wanted nothing to do with the kid, now I'll do whatever it takes to keep that little boy.

OAKLEY

It's six am and I'm sucking down my third cup of coffee. I'm going to need it to get through the day.

I haven't slept. Neither has Walker. We spent all night holding vigil over a sleeping little boy.

Micky.

He still hasn't spoken much, single words here and there, but it's progress.

After Shelby and Gannon returned last night with enough clothes to fill a wardrobe, blankets and sheets, and snacks as well as personal care items like soap and shampoo, toothbrush and paste, we set out making a room up for him.

He smiled a lot more when Gannon and Walker opened the big box filled with toys.

I have no idea how Gannon and Shelby managed to get all they did at that hour of night but I'm grateful because without them we'd still be floundering.

"You leave me any of that?" Walker asks as he enters the kitchen.

"Yeah, made a second pot."

He's freshly showered and I'm pushing to my feet and finding a place within his arms.

"Everything okay?" he murmurs against my temple.

"Yes. Just need a hug."

"I can give you that." He squeezes me. "I hope I'm the only one giving you them."

"I got a call from Pa."

"Oh?"

"He's got us a meeting with a judge here. We can't take Micky home—out of state—until we have him legally in our care."

"You hear from Amos?"

"Yes. She's not his co-guardian, and as far as he can find she has no connection to your cousin or his late wife."

"Then how the hell did she get involved in this? Wait. Late wife?"

"She died in childbirth having Micky."

"Fuck! He's got no one?"

"Yes, he does. He has you. Me. Shelby. And his mom's grandmother."

"Where the hell is the grandmother?"

"In a home but from what Amos has found she still gets out and about with help. He also found who Micky has been with for the last few months."

Pulling back, he looks down at me. "Who? How is Kristina connected to them."

"It's the woman who used to babysit Micky while your cousin worked. She's the one who connected with Kristina."

"How?"

I hated having to tell him this. It'll piss him off and lay a boatload of guilt on his shoulders. "Sara, the woman who's been taking care of Micky, came to your apartment months ago looking for you. She found Kristina instead."

"So she what? Left him with her?"

"No. From what I know so far, Sara didn't leave him, she took him back home with her. Amos is going to see her this morning. See if he can find out more of the details, but it looks like she had him until the day before yesterday when Kristina turned up and took him. Brought him here."

"Jeez, this is seriously crazy. I will never be able to thank you for sticking through all this." He shakes his head. "I won't blame you if you want to back out—"

I slap a hand over his mouth. "Don't you say it. I would never desert you. *Never.*"

"But we've only just gotten together," he murmurs against my palm.

"Don't care. You don't tell someone you love them, then hightail it out of there when shit gets hard. I am not my father."

His eyes go round, his eyebrows hiking up his forehead as those last five words echo in my head.

"Huh." I lower my hand from his face. "Didn't see that before."

"It's why you're the way you are." He lets me go to cradle my face. "You're loyal to the bone, Oakley. I get that more every day I'm with you, but I want you to know I'd understand—"

"Stop talking!"

He smiles at me. "Okay. But can I say one more thing?"

"What?" I eye him suspiciously.

"I love you."

I nod. "Okay, I'll allow that."

"Hungry."

We pull apart to find a sleep rumpled Micky standing a few feet away.

Crouching down so I'm at eye level with him, I ask, "What would you like to eat?"

"Pancake."

I glance up at Walker. "We can make pancakes."

"We can." Walker gets busy finding what we need. "I think Shel got one of those, yes, here it is." He holds up a box of pancake mix.

"What do you like on your pancakes, Micky?" I reach out a hand and hold my breath while I wait to see if he'll take it.

"Yellow sauce."

I look at Walker, and see he's got no more clue than me what yellow sauce is. "Okay, why don't you come over here and show me?"

I'm still looking at Walker when I feel a small warm hand slip into mine. My gaze zips back to Micky, to our hands, up to his face again.

He's smiling at me. A sleepy one and maybe when he wakes up more, he'll be wary of us again, but right now he's not, and I'll take that for the precious gift it is.

Leading him to the pantry, I move him in front of me so he can see what's on the shelves. He's way too short to see all of them.

"Can I pick you up so you can see?" I ask.

"Please."

His s is slurred a little but I think that's age more than a lisp. Gently I wrap my arms around him and put him on my hip. Taking in a deep breath, I swallow to clear my throat of the lump blocking it.

"Can you see the yellow sauce?"

Micky's arm shoots out, his finger pointed straight at the bottle of honey.

"Ah, right, yellow sauce." I grin as I grab the bottle and turn. I stop short when I see Walker standing there staring at us. I can't quite read the look in his eyes but I see the sheen of tears in them.

"Hey, little man, do you want to help me make the pancakes?"

When Micky nods, Walker holds out his arms and the weight on my hip shifts as Micky leans toward him.

With reluctance and pleasure I release my hold and follow them to the counter where Walker has everything set up ready to go.

"Need my help?" I ask.

"No. Why don't you jump in a quick shower while us men get breakfast ready?"

I see the concern in his eyes, know he's not as sure about being left alone with Micky as his words imply. "I'll only be a minute."

Walker nods and sits Micky on the counter. Picking up the pancake mix he asks, "You want to tip this in the bowl for me?"

The grin on Micky's face has my heart aching. I want to be sure he smiles like that all the time. I know I can't. Life dictates we can't smile all the time and if anyone has learned that, it's this little boy.

He's lost his mother, now his father, and he's only three.

My breath stalls.

Micky is the same age I was when Pa and Grams took me to live with them.

Glancing at Walker, I see his eyes darting between me and Micky. He places a hand on the little guy then turns to face me. With one eyebrow raised, he mouths, "You okay?", and I can't stop the smile forming.

With a quick nod, I bounce up on my toes and kiss his cheek. "Be back in a minute."

My shower is super quick, and I'm dressed even quicker. I've spent the last week wanting to be with Walker every second, and now with Micky in the picture, that desire is deeper, stronger.

I can't explain the connection except maybe the similarities between me and the little boy are what's binding us.

I hope today is simple, that we'll get to pack up and take Micky home tonight. I want him to meet Pa and I want to show him where he's going to live.

God. I know I'm getting ahead of myself. I know this isn't a done deal in spite of Walker's cousin naming him guardian. There's so much we don't know about the situation but that all takes a backseat to making sure Micky is safe.

With us.

When I make it back to the kitchen it's to the sound of little boy laughter and the deep rumble of Walker's masculine one.

Stopping on the threshold, I watch the two of them. Walker is making funny faces and Micky is laughing so hard if it wasn't for Walker's hand on his belly, he'd fall off the counter.

"What are you two doing?" I ask with a smile.

"Poop!" Micky shouts. "He made poop!"

"Ah." I look at Walker with an eyebrow arched.

"Pancake poop." His words do nothing to clarify what's so funny. "I was trying to make a pancake in the shape of a hockey puck, and let me say I think I got it, but this guy here says it's a poop."

"Oh, let me see." I move closer and when the pan comes into view, I struggle to hide my smile. "Well…"

Walker hooks his arm around my neck. "Don't say it."

I'm giggling now.

"Don't laugh either or I'll have to tickle you like I tickled this one." He wraps an arm around Micky and pulls him off the counter onto his hip. "Let's get the table set so I can make more hockey pucks."

Twisting out from under his arm, I put both hands on his back and say, "Why don't you two get the table sorted and I'll finish the pancakes."

Both my boys, and yes, they're my boys now—I refuse to think of them any other way—look at me with skepticism.

"Go, go. I've got this." I shoo them out of the kitchen. "And when you've got the table set, wash your hands," I call after them.

Damn. That sounded so mom-like. We might fumble through the next few months, hell, probably the next few years, but we'll make it through, and we'll do everything in our power to make sure Micky has the best life.

One his mom and dad would have given him but can't.

———

I'm looking at Judge Morgan in absolute shock. Beside me Walker isn't as dumbstruck.

"She did what? How the hell could she do that?"

"It's a simple process—"

Walker waves his arm to stop the explanation. "Okay, I get that, it wasn't really what I was asking."

"Ah, a rhetorical question?"

"No. I mean, how could she take my name?"

"You can change your name to whatever you want."

"Well, sure, I guess I get that but..."

His words trail off. Which is when I interject. "So she can change her name to Mrs. Kristina Alcott and tell people she's his wife?"

"Yes, and no. The name change, yes, the second no, and the paperwork that she had confirming that is fraudulent."

"Of course, it is! I didn't marry the woman!"

I place a hand on Walker's arm. "Calm down, we all know that." Facing the judge again I ask, "Can we press charges for anything she's done?"

"Yes. The fake marriage certificate is fraud and the fact she took the child and dropped him off in the foyer of your building is child endangerment I would think. I'm not sure about that—it's not my area of expertise."

"Okay, so we should get the police involved?"

"Yes. I can have someone call them for you. I think I saw Detective Alvarez in the hallway before you arrived. Give me a second."

He picks up the phone on his desk and talks quietly into it.

Turning to Walker, I lower my voice and say, "We're okay to take Micky home. I'll get us on a plane as soon as we leave here."

"We might need to stay and talk to the police."

"No. They can call us after we file the complaint." I think about that. "If that's even what we do. I don't know but I'm sure they will let us take him home. He's been through so much."

"Whatever we need to do to keep Micky safe."

"At least we know no one can take him away from you."

"True." He scrubs a hand through his hair. "I just wish I'd known about him when Michael was killed. Hell, I wish I'd known before that. Shelby and I would have helped him with Micky."

"You're here now and you're helping in a way your cousin would be eternally grateful for."

"I need to know everything. Where Michael lived, what is left of his things… the bag of clothes Micky had with him can't be the only ones he has."

"No. I'm sure they're not. I've got Amos on that."

I called the PI before we left the apartment to come here. He was already on the way to talk to Sara, and I asked him to find out everything he could from the woman.

Leaning over, Walker presses his mouth to mine. "I love you," he says against my lips.

"Love you too."

He kisses me quick and pulls back. "We're getting married the second we get home."

I grin. "Pa's already working on that. He's also got someone coming in to check the cubby house and swing set left from when I was a kid. He'll replace them if necessary."

"Was he excited about Micky?"

"More than. He's talking about letting him pick which room he wants and letting him decorate it. And something about a trip to the toy store."

Walker frowns. "We can't replace his parents."

"No. But he'll never doubt he's wanted and loved." The words are my personal vow to him. Speaking of vows… "I want him to be part of the wedding somehow."

"He can be my best man."

"Yes, if you want but I was thinking more of saying vows to him as well as you. It might take a few months for the official adoption paperwork to go through but he'll be ours in heart and life, long before he legally is."

"We can do that. And I mean we. I'll make vows for both of you too. We'll start our marriage and our family the same day."

"We kind of already have."

"I know, but this will be special, in front of our closest family and friends, a party to celebrate."

"We've got a lot to celebrate."

"We do. Us, Micky, the Rogues."

"Let's plan something to combine all of those things."

"You don't want to wait and do something separate for the Rogues?"

"At present the Rogues aren't really a team. We've got a few things in place, some people employed but other than the construction crew building what Pa keeps referring to as Rogue city, there's just me, Nat, Blake, and Cami. And you. And you aren't official yet."

"We'll fix that as soon as we're back in Baton Rouge. Nat has been going back and forth with Drake and my lawyer the last few days. They've ironed out everything. I just have to sign the contract when we get back."

"Good. I was beginning to think I'd need to resort to under-handed tactics to get your signature." I grin.

"Oh yeah, what kind of tactics?" Walker palms my face and brings our lips closer together again.

"The kind where I don't let you do what I see in your eyes."

He laughs. "Never. You'll never deny me because you'd just be denying yourself. Besides, you can't resist me."

"True. True. But it would be fun to try."

His eyes take on the deeper blue of arousal, the pupils dilating. "Hmm...maybe we should give it a try. See which one of us wins."

Now I'm laughing. "We're both winners in this."

"Yes, we are." He presses a kiss to my forehead before sitting back in his seat, his hand seeking mine. "In a week I've gone from feeling like a loser to the luckiest guy in the world."

Bringing my hand to his mouth, he kisses the ring he placed on my finger before we left the apartment.

"Yep. Luckiest guy in the world."

WALKER

The squeals of a happy three-year-old aren't what I expected at my wedding. But they're a welcome sound, far better than the music filtering through the outdoor speakers hidden in the garden beds around the backyard.

"Hey." Oakley bumps her hip against mine and I lift my arm for her to slide under it. "What are you doing?"

"Watching." I tip my chin in the direction of Micky and Pa.

"Oh."

We've been home three days and Micky has settled in so well no one would guess he hasn't lived here his whole life.

He and Pa are thick as thieves and getting into all kinds of things together. Today it's the slide attached to the new two-story cubby house that was delivered yesterday afternoon.

I don't know how we managed to keep either of them from seeing it until today. But the joy on both their faces was worth it.

"Amos called."

"Yeah?" I take my eyes off Micky to look at Oakley.

"They charged her with fraud and child endangerment."

"Thank fuck." I turn and wrap myself around my wife. "I hope they lock her up with a cellmate named Bertha."

Oakley laughs and pokes my side. "Who's getting bloodthirsty now? I thought that was my role in this relationship."

"When it comes to you and Micky being threatened, I'll always be bloodthirsty. Besides, someone wise once told me the best partnerships aren't one for one. They're about balance and in the most successful relationships that balance tips back and forth."

"Hmm...I wonder who this wise woman was?" She grins up at me. "In other news, we're heading out tomorrow."

"We are? I thought we were going to wait and go on our honeymoon later."

"Oh, this isn't that. We're going with Blake to Parry Sound then we'll head to Michael's to pack up more of Micky's things."

I blow out a breath. "Do you think we should take him back there so soon?"

"Yes. Sara will meet us there with her two. She said Micky can play at her house if we don't want him underfoot but I think we'll get her to stay at Michael's with us so she can tell us about their life."

"Okay. Is Pa coming with us? He mentioned wanting to thank Sara for looking after Micky."

I still can't believe Kristina told the woman I couldn't take Micky due to my injury but I'm glad he was with someone familiar for those months after his father died. I shudder when I think about the possibility of Kristina taking him back then.

"I think so, but I'll ask him." Her gaze moves to the swing set where Micky is now yelling for Pa to push him higher. "Although, I'm not sure we could separate them."

"No. They've been glued to each other since we came home."

"Do you mind?"

"What?" My gaze comes back to her. "Mind that Micky is smiling and talking? No, I don't mind at all."

"I meant that Pa is monopolizing all Micky's time."

"No. They won't have that forever. And Micky deserves someone totally devoted to him right now."

"Pa is definitely devoted." She smiles over at them. "I haven't seen him this happy since Grams was alive."

I hold her tighter and press my lips to the top of her head. "Have I told you how much I love you today, Mrs. Alcott?"

"Yes, Mr. Alcott, you have, but I'll happily listen to you tell me again." Tipping her head up, her gaze meets mine. "When."

Anyone else would be confused by that one word. Me? I know what she's asking for and I give it to her.

Slow and sweet and a little un-PG.

"Hey, get a room!"

Lifting my head, I see Pa grinning at us. The man hasn't just accepted Micky into his home, he's welcomed me with just as much enthusiasm.

And so far, there haven't been any issues having all of us under one roof but it's early days yet. I was prepared to move out with Micky except neither Pa nor Oakley were having any of that.

In Oakley's words, home is where the heart is and hers was with all of us so it makes sense to live together.

I'm not sure if it does make sense but I'm not arguing. I want to be with Oakley and in spite of the little boy who has been thrust into our lives, that hasn't changed, won't change.

"Hey, what has you frowning?" Her hand on my jaw pulls me back to face her. "What's wrong?"

"Are you sorry we did it like this?"

"What? Got married with just us here? No. Are you?"

"Hell no, I'd marry you in the living room in my boxers."

Laughing, she tips up on her toes and presses her lips to mine. "Well, good thing we didn't do it that way. After what happened when we met, Hot Stuff, I'm not sure I could trust you'd be wearing any."

Grinning, I slap her butt. "I replaced them."

"You did. Still..." She bites her bottom lip and has all sorts of thoughts racing through my head.

"Oh, you'd like it if I wasn't wearing any?"

"Maybe."

"Well, you're in luck. I may have a surprise wedding present for you later."

Her gaze drops. "You didn't. You aren't."

When her eyes come back to mine, I see they're dilated, and I smile. "You'll just have to wait for your wedding night to find out."

Before she has a chance to check, because I wouldn't put it past her to shove her hand down my pants to do that, I slip from her hold and head for the swings.

OAKLEY

"He wouldn't."

I stare at my husband's ass and try to determine if he's winding me up or not. I can't tell. I'm not sure if his underwear shows through his pants normally or not.

In the two weeks we've been together, he's gone without a number of times. Although in recent days he's been more conscious of the little boy now living with us.

I've been the same. Not to mention we also share a house with Pa. Both those things have put a crimp in our sex life. Not much but enough that when we find ourselves alone and able to indulge, we tend to crash together.

Not that we weren't doing that before...

Who am I kidding, we're still fucking like crazy, just not as randomly as before. Now we have to time things or sneak off so we don't get caught. The last thing we want is to get caught going at it.

I grin thinking about our first night here when Micky had a nightmare and screamed at the top of his lungs while Walker and I were in the middle of getting off.

How neither of us ended up with an injury that night is beyond me. We'd both been yanking on clothes as we'd raced down the hall to Micky's room. Talk about thrown in the deep end of parenthood.

Speaking of being parents, watching Walker play with a smiling Micky brings tears to my eyes.

Man and child may have had a rocky start, but things quickly evened out. I'm crediting the poop pancakes for that.

"I love that smile."

I turn to Pa. "I love yours."

"He's a hoot. We're going to get up to all sorts of mischief together."

"Good thing you're rich and can afford bail money then."

Laughing, Pa wraps his arm around my shoulders and tugs me close. "I wish your Grams was here to see this."

"Me too."

"She'd be so proud of you. Hell, she was proud of you, and you hadn't taken over the world yet."

"I haven't now."

"No, but you're getting there."

"I don't want the whole world, Pa."

"No, just a few parts of it."

"This new part is going to be the best part."

"The Rogues? Or those two?"

Smiling, I lean my head on his shoulder. "Those two."

"Are you happy, Annie?"

"Yes."

"Good. I'm about to make you happier."

"Oh?"

"Yep, I'm taking my new partner out for ice cream. Give the newlyweds some time alone."

"You don't need to do that."

"Who said anything about need? I want me a double scoop of chocolate chip cookie dough and I've got a youngster to corrupt."

"Good thing Grams isn't here or she'd be swatting you with the wooden spoon." I laugh.

"She used to chase us right out the front door when I told her I was taking you out to corrupt."

"And she did it with the biggest grin on her face."

"She did. She did."

"Should I take up the tradition?"

"Nah, we'll start a new one."

"Oh?"

"You bring 'em home, I'll corrupt 'em."

"You know you're the reason we named our clothing line Rogue, don't you?"

"Me?" Pa puts a hand to his chest.

"Yes. Grams used to call you a rogue all the time. Said you were one because it didn't matter what was expected or should be done, you went your own way. It's how we came up with the tagline too."

"Well." His eyes sparkle with moisture. "I'm honored and a little peeved you haven't told me before now. Think of all the bragging rights I've missed out on."

I laugh. "You've got enough to brag about."

"The only thing I have that deserves to be crowed about is you." He pulls me in for a full hug. "I'm so damn proud of you and I don't care what anyone else says or thinks, marrying that man is the smartest thing you've ever done. He's your Grams."

"Yes. He is."

"Did we ever tell you I asked her to marry me the day we met?"

"No," I gasp, pulling back to look at him. "Why have I never heard that?"

"Don't know. But I knew she was mine the second I laid eyes on her. We were barely eighteen and it took me a good two years to convince her to marry me, but I got there."

"It's the James stubborn gene."

"It is. And as your Grams used to say, you've got it out the wazoo, Annie Oakley."

"Why did you call her that, Pa?"

We turn to see Walker and Micky have joined us. I look at Pa and nod. I'll let him tell the story—he always makes it sound better than me.

"Well, come here, young man, and let me tell you a tale about a little girl not much older than you and her love of water pistols." He slips his hand into Micky's then says, "We'll be heading out for a treat and story time."

"Single scoop. I don't want either of your spoiling your appetites."

He looks at his watch. "Double, one hour for each scoop to digest and we'll be ready for dinner." He gives me a wink before he leads Micky into the house.

"I want to worry about spoiling him but I don't think it'll hurt if we do for a little while." Walker slips his arm around me as we watch them go. "How long do we have?"

Turning, I put both hands on his chest and tip my head back. "Long enough for you to show me what you've got on under those pants, Hot Stuff."

Laughing, he bends, and before I work out what he's doing, I'm looking at the back of his legs, my face bouncing off his hard butt as he jogs into the house.

OAKLEY

Standing in the driveway I glance over at Walker. "You sure this is where he's staying?"

"Yep," he says with a nod, but the frown has me worried.

"Hmm..."

"I know what you're thinking."

"Do you?" I doubt it but we'll see.

"Yes. He hasn't played in over a year and the last time he hit the ice, his blood alcohol level could have felled a buffalo."

I smile. "I'm not thinking about any of that."

Walker looks at me with one brow arched high.

"I'm wondering if we'll have to break down the door and if we do, will I get a splinter."

He shoves a hand into his jacket pocket and comes out with a key. And the cocky grin I love. "Nope."

"Where did you get that?" We start up the drive toward the door.

"Gannon gave it to me before we left New York last time we were there."

"Oh. Right. I forgot this was his house. Does he know what state it's in?"

"The outside looks a little shabby, but I promise, it's not as bad as it looks." Walker lets me and Blake up the stairs to the door first.

"We'll see."

When our knock goes unanswered, Walker uses the key to open the door.

Stepping inside, I'm surprised by how clean the place is, and light. The back part of the house has lots of windows and you can see the woods behind the house from the foyer.

Moving deeper into the house I'm beginning to think no one is home when a prone figure on the floor on the other side of the couch grabs my attention.

Thinking the worst, I race around only to come up short when I see the bottle on the floor.

"That doesn't bode well," I mutter. Picking up the bottle I see it's three quarters empty and set it on the coffee table.

I look to Walker and Blake but neither says a word. They're both looking at the man at my feet.

Moving my gaze back down, I stare at our supposed hot shot sprawled on the floor. I want to turn around and walk right out of here but I have to defer to my coaches.

"Are we sure?"

"Yes." Walker doesn't hesitate. "Positive."

"I'll second that."

I glance back at Blake. She's been suspiciously quiet since we pulled up in front of the ramshackle house Branton Lattimer calls home. "Really? It's going to be you fixing this mess."

"Yep." Blake pops the p.

"Okay." Looking around, I can't see what I'm looking for. "Give me a minute."

I leave them there, both studying the man we've come to talk to.

The one who I'm sure is currently in an alcoholic coma. We're about to find out if it's a deadly one.

Finding the utility room, I open all the cupboards before I find what I'm after.

A bucket.

Bucket in hand, I head to the kitchen and hope I find the second ingredient to my wake the drunk ass up remedy.

Yanking the fridge door open I find a surprisingly clean space with fresh food. "Hmm…someone is looking after the guy."

"What are you doing?"

I glance up. I didn't hear Walker come in. "Looking for cold water."

"You're thirsty?" He shakes his head.

"No." Going back to the fridge I search the bottles in the door before moving onto the shelves. Dammit. Looks like it will be tap water. I was hoping for something colder but it will do.

When I make it back to the living room and the man on the floor, Walker and Blake are huddled together on the far side of the room whispering.

Why is anyone's guess and something I'm not concerned about. It isn't like the man can hear anything right now. He's still out cold.

Not for long.

Gripping the handle tight with one hand, I place the other on the bottom of the bucket and tip it.

Right on Branton Lattimer's head.

He comes up swinging and cursing and I jump back to get out of the way.

"Jesus fucking Christ!" He wipes a large hand down his face. "Who the hell are you?"

"Your savior or your worst nightmare."

"Huh?" He shakes like a dog, spraying water droplets all around him. "What?"

"Your savior or your worst nightmare. You choose." If I were being honest, I'd tell him I'm probably going to be both.

"Bran." Walker moves next to me.

"Cap? What the hell?"

"When did you eat last?" Walker asks, while offering a hand.

"Dunno. What time is it?"

"Almost midday."

Branton eyes me. "What day?"

I suck in a breath and hope to hell my coaches aren't steering me wrong here. "Thursday."

"Huh." Branton looks around the room before his gaze settles on the coffee table. "Not even one bottle."

I'm not sure why he's pointing that out. It's more than enough for me to worry about taking this guy on.

"How are you doing, Bran?" Walker pointedly stares at the bottle.

Branton laughs. "You think I'm drunk all the time?" Shaking his head, he tugs his shirt over it and slaps his abs. "Do these look like I live on alcohol?"

I have to admit he's in good shape. At least it looks that way.

Walker smiles. "Wanna put those to good use?"

"Doing?" Branton asks with a raised brow.

"Playing."

"Ha! Like any team is going to want me after what I did."

"The Rogues want you." My words snap out. "We need someone with your skills and experience to guide us to the finals."

"Who the hell are the Rogues?"

"The new NHL franchise." Walker claps him on the shoulder. "I want you on my team."

"You're playing for them? When did you leave New York?"

"When Blanchett slammed me into the boards and left me unable to play at a professional level."

"Wait. You're not playing? Then how the hell would I be on your team?"

"I'm head coach."

Branton and Walker stare at each other for long seconds before Branton breaks the stare and turns to me. "And who the hell are you? The general manager?"

"No. That's Natalie Redding. I'm the team owner and this" —I wave my hand toward Blake who's been hiding in the back corner—"is our assistant coach, Blake Watts."

Branton spins on his heel so fast he stumbles but the commotion isn't enough to mask the gasped, "Blake," that leaves his mouth.

I watch as my best friend and Branton have a conversation with their eyes only and I make a mental note to ask her about it later.

There's history here I'm unaware of.

"I…" Branton takes a step toward her. "Blake."

Her name holds so much anguish, it tightens my chest.

"Bran."

The next thing I know Branton launches across the room and wraps his arms around her. He burrows his face in her neck and the tightening in my chest goes to lung crushing as his sobs fill the room.

A quick look at Walker and we make a mutual decision to leave them and head for the front door.

Once outside, the door closed behind us, I ask, "You know about that?"

"They used to be close. Before…"

"Ah."

"And Bran is—was—really close to her brothers, the twins."

"Right. Of course. I saw that in his report. Just never made the connection to Blake."

"There were rumors before he got married. About him and her. But they never admitted to being in a relationship other than friends."

"Will their history be a problem?"

"No. She's solid and he's not about to let their past affect him."

"Just his own past."

"I don't know the whole story, but I know he only got married because of the baby."

"Well fuck."

Branton's story is tragic on so many levels and I'm not aware of all of them, I'm sure.

I still don't know if he's what we need. Losing a child has to be devastating.

Now I have Micky, and it's only been a few days, I don't think I'd be able to come back from that kind of loss.

I have no idea how Branton Lattimer is still breathing.

"Oakley."

I turn to see Blake in the doorway. "Yeah."

"I'm staying. Give me a few days and I'll let you know if we need to keep looking or if Bran is joining us."

"You're staying here?"

"For now."

"Should I worry about you? What that was about?"

Shaking her head, she gives me a small smile. "No. We're good. I'm good."

"I don't want to leave if—"

"I'll be fine. Bran isn't who the media has made him out to be."

"No one ever is." I take a deep breath. "Okay, keep me posted. If I don't hear from you in…three days I'm coming back."

"You won't have to. Promise."

Going up the steps, I pull her in to hug and say, "Call for anything, doesn't have to be about the Rogues."

"Thanks. Safe trip home." When she pulls away, she waves to Walker and says, "See you later, Cap."

"Cap?"

"It's what Bran called him. I forgot he was the captain of the Knights. See you both later."

I watch her slip back inside and close the door.

Turning to Walker, I say, "Well, Hot Stuff, I guess we wait to see if we've got ourselves a hot shot…"

———

Hockey hot shot Branton Lattimer is fighting to reclaim his life

on and off the ice. Falling for his best friend's older sister—*his coach*—makes that battle seem impossible.
Read HOT SHOT, book two in the HOT AS PUCK series.

For what's coming next, latest releases, sales and more, join
Rhian's Royal Readers
http://www.rhiancahill.com/contact/newsletter/

If you enjoyed this book, please consider leaving a review. It only takes a few minutes and you'll be helping other readers find stories they'll enjoy, as well as supporting authors you love.

Acknowledgments

It's always scary to release a new book, more so when you haven't released anything new in a while, but throw a life changing event into the mix and things get even scarier.

This is my first *fully new* post-breast cancer book and I've added more anxiety to the mix by writing in a sub-genre I haven't before. I've also moved from 3rd person to 1st and let me say, releasing Hot Stuff is one hell of a nail biting moment for me.

Walker and Oakley were a joy to write and I can't wait to share the rest of the Rogues and their paths to true love with the world.

I thank you from the bottom of my soul (this is way too big for just my heart) for taking a chance on me and this book.

xoxo

Rhian

About Rhian Cahill

Rhian Cahill is the alter ego of a former stay-at-home mother of four. With motherly duties rapidly dwindling, Rhian is able to make use of the fertile imagination she used to keep herself sane for all those years of slavery. Years spent living overseas and visiting tropical climates have helped inspire some steamy stories.

Multi-published in erotic romance, paranormal romance, and contemporary romance, Rhian, with the help of Mr. Muse, spends her days and nights writing.

When not glued to the keyboard you'll find her, book or knitting in hand, avoiding any and all housework as much as possible.

For more on Rhian –

Website – http://www.rhiancahill.com/
Newsletter signup – http://www.rhiancahill.com/contact/newsletter/
FaceBook – https://www.facebook.com/RhianCahillAuthor
Instagram – http://instagram.com/rhiancahill/
Twitter – https://twitter.com/RhianCahill
BookBub – https://www.bookbub.com/authors/rhian-cahill
Goodreads – https://www.goodreads.com/rhian_cahill

OTHER TITLES BY RHIAN CAHILL

CONTEMPORARY ROMANCE

Hot as Puck

Hot Stuff

Hot Shot

Hot Damn

Hot Puck

Hot Hook

Hot Date

Love Beach

Summer With a Fake Date

Merry With a Scrooge

Spring Break With a Baby Daddy

Evergreen Lake

Jingle Balls

Winter Lake Series

Love Me Like You Do

Love The Way You Are

When You Love Someone

Let Me Love You

Wild Rush Of Love

Party Games Series

Truth Or Dare

Spin The Bottle

Pass The Parcel (novella)

Are You Game? Series

7 Minutes In Heaven

Catch'n'Kiss

Red Light, Green Light

Hearts Are Wild Series

No More Talking (novella)

Dare You To (novella)

Mad Love

Boys Of Summer

Bondi Beach Boys

Sand, Surf And Sunnie

Only You Series

All Of You

Holiday Romances

Christmas Wishes

New Year's Kisses

Valentine's Dates

Secret Santa

Frosty's Snowmen Series

A Touch Of Frost

A Kiss From Kringle

A Taste For Kandy

Hot and Bothered

Doing Logan

Shut Up And Kiss Me

PARANORMAL ROMANCE

Coyote Hunger Series

Coyote Home

Coyote Wild

Coyote Whispers

Coyote Law (novella)

Coyote Lies

For a full list of available books visit

http://www.rhiancahill.com/books/

For what's coming next, latest releases, sales and more, join

Rhian's Royal Readers

http://www.rhiancahill.com/contact/newsletter/